Blood Relative

I tossed the cotton pad at the garbage can, but missed. I bent to pick it up. That's when I noticed a smear of red on the white plastic garbage liner. It looked like . . . blood!

Frowning, I shook the edge of the can to shift the contents. A crumpled tissue rolled to one side and I spotted a small plastic bottle labeled TRANSPARENT NONDRYING STAGE BLOOD. It was empty but for a few drops.

I crouched there on my heels, trying to understand what I was seeing. Stage blood? Why was there an empty bottle of stage blood in our bathroom?

Suddenly I flashed back to Kelly's flushed face and furtive manner as she slipped back into the reception room after the animal-rights protesters were hauled away. The animal-rights protesters who'd been made up with gallons of stage blood.

Had Kelly had something to do with that protest? It seemed as though nothing else could explain the stage blood in the garbage can.

Why on earth would Kelly want to sabotage her own father's company?

NANCY DREW

Available from Aladdin Paperbacks

CAROLYN KEENE

NANCY DREW

GIRL DETECTIVE®

PERFECT COVER

#31

**Book Two in the
Perfect Mystery Trilogy**

CAROLYN KEENE

Aladdin Paperbacks
New York   London   Toronto   Sydney

❧ ALADDIN PAPERBACKS
An imprint of Simon & Schuster Children's Publishing Division
1230 Avenue of the Americas, New York, NY 10020
Copyright © 2008 by Simon & Schuster, Inc.
All rights reserved, including the right of
reproduction in whole or in part in any form.
NANCY DREW, NANCY DREW: GIRL DETECTIVE, ALADDIN PAPER-
BACKS, and related logo are registered trademarks of Simon & Schuster, Inc.
Manufactured in the United States of America
First Aladdin Paperbacks edition July 2008
10 9 8 7 6 5 4 3 2 1
Library of Congress Control Number 2007934378
ISBN-13: 978-1-4169-5530-6
ISBN-10: 1-4169-5530-5

Contents

PERFECT COVER

NEW YORK, NEW YORK, IT'S A WONDERFUL TOWN

"Ladies and gentlemen," the flight attendant announced over the intercom, "we've begun our final descent into New York City. Please make sure your seat belts are fastened and your seat backs and tray tables are in the upright and locked position."

"Look out, New York, Nancy Drew is here. Yes, I mean *that* Nancy Drew, teen detective and beauty pageant winner!" George Fayne, one of my two closest friends, turned to me from the aisle seat and held an imaginary microphone to her lips. "The-e-e-ere she is, Mi-iss Pretty Face . . . ," she crooned.

I groaned. "George, if you sing that to me one

more time, I swear I'll seal your mouth with duct tape."

George smirked. "Goes with the territory, Nan. I know you entered the Miss Pretty Face pageant to solve a mystery, but the mystery's over now—and yet, here you are, about to take part in the next phase of the competition. I just want to hear you admit that you're a real pageant girl."

"I am not!" I protested. "It just didn't seem right to drop out, especially after all the drama the pageant has had the last couple of years."

I'd originally entered the regional Miss Pretty Face beauty pageant to go undercover. I had been trying to find out why the previous year's winner had been dethroned. I solved that mystery, and found plenty of scandals and surprises along the way—but the biggest surprise came when I ended up winning the pageant! Now I was on my way to New York City to represent our hometown, River Heights, in the nationwide Miss Pretty Face pageant. George and my other best friend, George's cousin Bess Marvin, had come with me for moral support (or, in George's case, to torture me in person) and to take a vacation in the big city.

The plane's wheels touched down on the runway and we taxied toward our gate.

"Nancy, can I borrow your Perfect Face again?" Bess asked.

I laughed. "I know you just want to borrow some lotion, but it sounds weird when you put it that way. I feel like saying, 'My face doesn't come off!'" Unzipping my carry-on bag, I looked inside for the small Perfect Face Revitalizing Lotion samples I had been given as a contestant. "You can have them all," I said, handing them to her. "To be honest, I don't really like the way the lotion makes my face feel."

"Oooh, I do," Bess said, smoothing it onto her cheeks. "I totally love it! It's so tingly."

"That's exactly why I don't like it," I told her. "I don't know, it just feels strange."

George put a finger to her lips. "Shhh, don't say anything bad about the Pretty Face products. Piper's listening," she cautioned me. "I bet she's trying to find some dirt on you so she can get you disqualified as Miss Pretty Face and take your place."

I sneaked a glance between the seat backs. Sure enough, in the row behind us, the first runner-up, a blond girl named Piper Depken, was leaning forward with her ear cocked. When she caught me looking at her, she flushed and leaned back, giving me a cold stare. "You've got bags under your eyes," she told me, then pointedly held up a magazine and pretended to read it.

I sighed. Talk about a change of attitude. When I first entered the pageant, Piper had been friendly and seemingly helpful, giving me advice about how to make myself a better beauty queen. Granted, her tips included telling me that I was ten pounds overweight and trying to convince me to go on an awful diet in order to lose the weight, but still. However, the moment it had become clear that I was actual competition, the friendly manner had vanished. Piper wanted to win the pageant crown, and she wanted it bad.

In fact, I did feel a bit guilty about winning. The crown happened to come with a lot of great stuff, like a scholarship, not to mention free Pretty Face cosmetics for life, since Pretty Face was the pageant's sponsor. Piper, I knew, came from a poor family and could really have used the scholarship.

"Oh, and Nancy?" Piper added, tapping my shoulder.

I turned around. "Yes?"

"That blue top? Wrong color for you," she said, and gave me a poisonously sweet smile.

On the other hand, I'd have felt much worse

if I'd taken the crown from somebody who was actually *nice*.

After we got off the plane and collected our bags, a sleek black limousine whisked us away toward the Manhattan skyline. Bess, George, Piper, and I shared the big car with Kyle McMahon, the North American brand manager of Pretty Face cosmetics, and his daughter, Kelly, who happened to be the previous year's Miss Pretty Face River Heights.

"Thanks for letting George and me share the limo, even though we're not in the pageant, Mr. McMahon," Bess gushed. "I feel like a queen, riding into Manhattan this way!"

Kyle McMahon had been scrolling through the e-mails on his PDA, but now he looked up and gave Bess a smile. "You're very welcome," he told her. "It's bending the rules a bit, but we had the room."

His cell phone rang and he answered the call. "Kyle McMahon here. . . . Yes, that's right. . . . No, that ad campaign rolls out next week. . . . Hang on, I've got the e-mail chain right here. . . ."

As he spoke, he massaged the bridge of his nose wearily. I caught Kelly's look of concern and gave her a sympathetic smile. "He works pretty hard, doesn't he?" I whispered.

"Especially since he got promoted. He was supposed to spend a week a month in New York City, but he's been here more like three weeks a month," Kelly whispered back. She pushed a strand of blond hair off her forehead. "I know I should be happy for him and all, but this new job is really stressing him out."

Kelly's mom had passed away when she was ten, and she was an only child, so the bond between her and her dad was pretty tight. I knew what that was like—I lost my mom when I was just a little kid, too—so I completely understood her concern.

"Things will settle down after the pageant is over," I told her.

"I hope so," she said with a sigh.

We wound through the crooked, tree-lined streets of Greenwich Village and finally pulled up in front of a sleek glass-and-steel building that towered over the surrounding brownstones. A uniformed bellhop came out and opened our car door. "Welcome to the Horatio, ladies," he said.

"The Horatio Hotel." Bess sighed in rapture. "I read all about this place in *Us* magazine. It's the hottest new spot in the city. I spent a week calling them four times a day until they had a cancellation and I could get a room." Since she wasn't with the pageant, Bess had gotten a separate room for George and herself.

"Wow," I murmured as I climbed out of the limo. It was certainly a far cry from the chain hotels where beauty pageants were typically held. "I wonder what kind of strings Pretty Face had to pull to get the whole pageant in here."

Kelly overheard me and gave me a slightly forced smile. "My dad is the one who made all the arrangements," she said. "Don't tell me you're thinking of investigating him!"

"No, no," I assured her quickly. "I didn't mean anything by it."

Whoops! Ever since I'd revealed that I was a detective, everyone in the pageant had been treating me a bit warily. It had been especially hard with Kelly because we'd gotten to be such good friends during the River Heights pageant and I think she felt blindsided when she found out I'd been keeping a secret from her.

"Well, that's a relief," Kelly said with a laugh.

We went inside and registered. I saw George's eyes widen as she looked at the room rates. Bess grinned mischievously. "Hottest spot in the city," she reminded George.

"Right," George said, gulping. "Remind me to point that out to my mom when she sees the bill."

Kelly and I followed the bellhop up to the eighth-floor room we were sharing. It was filled with light from a huge window that looked west over the Hudson River. "This is gorgeous!" I said, sinking down on one of the cream-colored armchairs. A low glass coffee table held a bouquet of pink-and-white flowers that filled the air with a delicious scent. I leaned back and stretched out my legs. "Why does traveling make me so tired? It's not like I did anything but sit all day, but I feel like I could just stay in this armchair forever. That is, if we can get something from room service. I'm starving!"

Kelly glanced at the pageant agenda that had been left in our room, then at her watch. "Sorry to burst your bubble, but the welcome reception starts in an hour," she told me. "We've just got time to unpack, freshen up, and change."

I got up, sighing. "A pageant girl's work is never done."

"Tell me about it," Kelly said with a laugh. "You know, I loved being Miss Pretty Face, but I have to say I'm glad it's your responsibility now. It's hard to be *on* all the time. And it's nice to know I can leave the reception any time I want."

As I rummaged through my cosmetics bag, I frowned. "Uh-oh. I gave all my Perfect Face samplers to Bess and I forgot to bring a big jar for myself. I'm not being a very good representative of Pretty Face!"

"Lucky for you I *am* a good one," Kelly joked, and held up her own jar of Perfect Face Revitalizing Lotion. It looked different from mine, as Kelly's dad was always giving her lab samples rather than the finished product, but I didn't care. All that mattered was that I show up wearing it. I took it with a smile of thanks and moved into the bathroom to put it on.

"Hey, Bess and George and I were thinking that after the reception we'd go out and see the town," I called to Kelly. "You want to come with?"

There was a long pause. Then Kelly said, "Um, I'm not sure."

I stuck my head into the bedroom. "What's up? You've got a hot date or something?" I teased.

Her cheeks turned pink. "Why would you think that? No, I just don't know whether I'll be too tired. It's been kind of a long day."

She seemed a little sensitive, so I backed off. "I know what you mean. The way I'm feeling right now, I might come back after the reception too. It *has* been a long day. And I've got a fitness class tomorrow morning."

An hour later the two of us met George and Bess at the elevators. "The reception is in the rooftop ballroom," Kelly said as we rode up. "It's supposed to have the most spectacular view of the city and New York Harbor."

I smoothed the front of my dark blue silk sheath dress. "Do I look okay?"

"Gorgeous," Bess told me, licking her finger and smoothing a stray lock of strawberry blond hair back into my up-do. Bess looked stunning as always in a floaty pink dress that set off her big blue eyes and blond hair. George had on a fitted charcoal cocktail dress that showed just how toned and athletic her figure is. She was fiddling with her new digital camcorder, which was tiny and sleek. George is a technology wiz—and a technology freak.

The elevator doors opened and all four of us gasped at the same moment. The rooftop ballroom *was* spectacular. It was all decorated in light wood, glass, and brushed steel, with a high ceiling and a giant skylight. Huge picture windows gave views of the city in every direction. Off to the south we could see the Statue of Liberty and the harbor, to the north the Empire State Building, the Brooklyn and Manhattan bridges to the east, and in the west the sun was just starting to set over New Jersey. At one end of the room was a small stage, where a jazz combo played softly.

The room was already crowded with well-dressed people. I spotted Piper by the northern window, wearing a deep red gown and chatting with a tall, willowy, dark-skinned girl who I guessed was one of the other regional Miss Pretty Faces. Kyle McMahon stood by the buffet, a glass in his hand, talking to a huge, muscular man with an iron-gray crew cut who looked as if he should be wearing an army uniform rather than the expensive-looking dark suit he had on.

"Buffet," I said, remembering how hungry I was. "I'm there!"

But Kyle had already spotted Kelly and was hurrying over to us, followed by the guy with the crew cut. "I just called your room and left a message," he told her. "I was starting to get worried."

I discreetly checked my watch. The reception had started at 7:00. It was now 7:07. And Kelly's dad was already worrying about her being late? Once again, I thanked my stars that my dad wasn't crazy overprotective with me like Kyle was with Kelly.

Bess and George moved off as Kyle gestured to the big man at his side. "Ladies, this is Adam Bedrossian, head of security for Pretty Face cosmetics," he told us. "Adam, this is my daughter, Kelly, the former Miss Pretty Face River Heights, and Nancy Drew, our current Miss Pretty Face."

"Security?" I repeated, startled. "You mean, like, a bodyguard?"

Adam Bedrossian smiled slightly and spoke in a deep, rumbling voice. "Most of the threats I deal with aren't physical, per se. More along the lines of keeping the corporation and its representatives out of trouble," he told me. "Although I was a Green Beret. So, Nancy Drew. I've heard about you. Heard you uncovered some problems with the River Heights pageant."

"That's me," I said.

His pale eyes, studying me, were cold. "I don't think you'll find any problems like that here. But if you do, I hope you'll bring them to me rather than trying to crack the case on your own."

I bristled a little. Something in the way he spoke was vaguely insulting. Or was I just imagining it? I get a lot of resentment from professionals in law enforcement and detective work because I'm an amateur.

"Don't worry," I said, deciding I was just being

oversensitive. "I'm not looking for any new cases. I'm just here to have fun and represent River Heights."

"Well-spoken," Kyle told me with a hearty laugh. "Now, if you'll excuse us. . . ." Taking Kelly's arm, he moved off through the crowd, still talking to Adam Bedrossian. Kelly cast me an apologetic look over her shoulder. I smiled and shrugged at her to show I understood.

Finally, I could make for the buffet! As I reached it, my stomach gave a loud growl. I glanced around in embarrassment, hoping no one had heard.

The petite, dark-haired girl next to me gave me a broad smile. "I know just how you feel," she said with a slight Spanish accent. "I've had my eye on the shrimp cocktail for the past ten minutes. I hope you're not planning on having any, or I may have to fight you for it."

I burst out laughing. "Don't worry, I'll stay far away from the shrimp," I promised, helping myself to some cheese and melon slices. "I'm Nancy Drew, by the way. Miss Pretty Face River Heights, believe it or not. Are you one of the contestants?"

The girl almost choked on her shrimp. "Me? Not quite," she said when she'd recovered. "I'm a biochemist. My name is Anna Chavez."

"Oh, too bad. I was hoping for someone normal among the other contestants," I blurted out. Then I felt my cheeks turn bright red. "Oh—I mean . . ."

Anna giggled. "I know what you mean. Believe me."

I liked Anna already. "I really didn't mean to offend anyone. It's just that I still feel a little out of place here. I'm not really a pageant girl, if you want to know the truth."

"Oh, that's why I recognized your name. I heard about you!" Anna said. "You're that detective who investigated last year's River Heights pageant, right? Nice job. I'm impressed that you're a detective—you're pretty young to be doing work like that."

"I was about to say the same thing about you. So what's it like being a biochemist? And what are you doing here at the Miss Pretty Face reception?" I asked.

Anna dipped a shrimp in cocktail sauce and ate it. "As for why I'm here, I work for Pretty Face here in New York. Research," she told me. "As for what that's like . . ." She grinned. "It's fantastic! I've got my dream job!"

"How did you get into it?" I asked.

Anna shrugged. "Science runs in my family, I suppose. My father was a botanist, back home in Venezuela, where I grew up. He used to take me on nature walks in the jungle all the time. We played a game where I had to identify plants, so I got to know the tropical botanicals quite well."

"I bet he's really proud of you now," I commented.

A shadow crossed her face. "He and my mother passed away when I was seventeen. Car accident."

I bit my lip. "I'm so sorry," I said. "Both your parents! That must have been hard."

"It was," she agreed. "I had no other family in Venezuela. Mama was an only child and Papa's sisters and their families live in England."

"So how did you end up here in the U.S.?" I asked. I hoped she didn't think I was being too nosy. I guess I'm just used to asking a lot of questions—it just goes along with doing detective work.

"My brother—he's fifteen years older than me—brought me to live with him, in Texas, where he works as a chemist for one of the oil companies," Anna explained. She ate another shrimp. "He got me a job working in his company, and I found out I loved chemistry as much as biology.

So I went to college and graduate school, and, well . . ." She spread out her hands. "Here I am. Pretty Face uses lots of tropical botanicals in its cosmetic formulas, and I know all about them from my father, so it was a perfect place for me to work."

"Wow!" I said. "That's an inspiring story."

"What is?" asked George, who'd just walked up with Bess. She held up her camcorder. "Smile, you two. You're being immortalized."

I introduced my friends to Anna and explained what she'd just told me.

"You can't be a biochemist!" Bess protested. "You're too young and pretty!"

"Well, thank you," Anna said, her eyes twinkling. "But I assure you, I am older than I look. I work on product development at Pretty Face."

"Obviously you've been trying out your own products," Bess said. "Your skin is absolutely flawless! You must use Perfect Face every day."

Anna hesitated. "Actually . . . ," she began.

But that was as far as she got. Because at that moment all the lights in the room went out. I caught my breath. There were cries of alarm in the dark all around me.

A distorted voice shrieked, "The murderers will be exposed!"

AN UGLY ACCUSATION

I clapped my hands to my ears as feedback whined through the room's speakers at top volume.

My eyes adjusted quickly to the dark, especially since there was still a lot of light coming in through the windows from the city outside. I could see shadowy figures darting around the stage area. A moment later green spotlights came up and lit the stage. Beside me, Bess let out a little cry and dug her fingers into my arm.

On the stage stood a line of hideously injured people. People with blood streaming down their faces from their eyes . . . people with bandages covering their ears . . . people with their lips stitched shut . . . My stomach turned over.

"This is what Pretty Face really looks like!" shrieked the same voice as before. It was so distorted it was impossible to tell whether it was male or female. "This is what *you* look like when you put their makeup on your faces! Did you know they test their products on helpless animals?"

"What in the . . . ," Anna muttered, and began pushing her way toward the stage. I followed her. As I got closer, I saw that the "blood" and "stitches" on the faces of the actors were crudely drawn on with stage makeup.

Before I could reach the stage, though, the green lights went out. I saw several burly figures rush forward and efficiently grapple the actors off the stage. "You can try to silence us, but the truth will come out!" the voice screeched. "The murderers—"

The speaker system crackled, then went dead. A second later the room lights blinked back on. By the door I spotted a knot of struggling people—a skinny guy with long, stringy hair and a wispy goatee, a pale-looking girl dressed all in black, and two or three others—who were clearly losing the altercation with the team of security guards. In a moment they were whisked out of the room. Adam Bedrossian hurried out after them, speaking into a handheld radio as he went.

The crowd was buzzing, people muttering and looking horrified. "Wow!" George murmured in my ear. "That was dramatic."

Kyle McMahon pushed forward and jumped on the stage. "Ladies and gentlemen!" he called. "Please accept our deepest apologies for the shocking and unpleasant disturbance. I would like to reassure everyone that we've already rounded up the agitators. I would also like to take this opportunity to categorically deny what was said. Pretty Face does not, never has, and never will test its products on animals, period. This is a cornerstone of our corporate philosophy. I don't know where these people got their information from, but it is malicious and completely false."

I frowned. Kyle's voice rang with sincerity. But if he was telling the truth, then why had the protesters said what they said? Why make an accusation like that if it wasn't true? Surely it would be easy enough to check.

"So please, folks," Kyle went on, "I know it's hard, but try to forget about this unpleasantness. Eat, drink, have a good time, and please believe me when I tell you there's not a grain of truth in what you just heard."

His words seemed to be having an effect. People were still buzzing excitedly, but much of the tension had gone out of the room.

I glanced around for Anna Chavez. If anyone was in a position to know the truth of the matter, she was. My eyes fell on Kelly, who was slipping into the room from one of the rear doors. Her cheeks looked flushed, as if she'd been running.

"That was weird," Bess announced. "I mean, Pretty Face is all about being eco-friendly. How could anyone accuse *them* of animal testing? It's like . . . like suggesting that Gucci uses fake leather in their shoes."

George ran her fingers through her short dark hair. "Well, if it was true, think of the scandal it would cause. It would destroy the company."

Hmm. I gnawed on my lip as I thought about that one. Maybe someone was out to smear Pretty Face's reputation. A rival cosmetics company, perhaps?

"Uh-oh," George said, reading my face correctly. "Nancy's sensing a mystery, aren't you, Nan?"

I grinned a bit sheepishly. "Maybe I am. Hard to say. I *would* like to ask a few questions."

Once again I looked around the room for

Anna. This time I spotted her, deep in conversation with Kyle McMahon. She was chopping the air with her hand as she gestured urgently. Adam Bedrossian stood a few steps behind Kyle, hands clasped in front of him, feet planted slightly apart in a classic tough-guy pose.

"Guess I better wait until they're finished talking," I said.

The willowy girl who'd been talking to Piper earlier came up to us, her hand fluttering on her chest. "Can you believe this?" she asked in a breathy voice. "It's just so crazy!"

We all introduced ourselves and I learned that her name was Alanna Davies and that she was Miss Pretty Face Seattle. Then Alanna beckoned over Miss Pretty Face Albuquerque, a petite brunette named Raven Yahzee. We all gossiped about the creepy protest for a while. Alanna and Raven both agreed with Bess that the protesters must be either insane or seriously ignorant.

When I looked for Anna again, she seemed to have left. Kyle was speaking to a white-haired woman in a spangly blue gown. Adam was over by one of the doors, speaking on his radio again.

Rats! I'd really wanted to talk to Anna. Well, I thought, I'll just have to track her down at her office tomorrow.

Gradually the mood of the party returned to normal. Alanna and Raven introduced me to the other regional Miss Pretty Faces—there were eight of us in all—and we all met the pageant coordinator, an immaculately dressed, slender man in his sixties named Harrison Hendrickson. He had a mane of silver hair, which he kept smoothing back with one manicured hand.

"I'll be seeing all of you young ladies bright and early tomorrow. I'm sure we're going to have *lots* of fun together," he said with a smile that didn't quite reach his eyes.

A little after ten, I made my way over to Bess and George again. George held up her camcorder. "The memory is full," she announced. "And I'm kind of wiped out. I don't think I'm up for a night on the town."

"Me, either," I agreed. "But I'm still starving! I mingled so much I barely got to touch the buffet. I say we go back to your guys' room and order room service."

"Careful," said a voice at my elbow. I turned to see Harrison Hendrickson standing behind me. He cast an appraising eye at me. "Eating at this hour is sure to cause bloating and weight gain. And that's something you really can't afford, sweet pea."

And, smiling that mechanical smile, he sauntered away.

"Ugh," George commented. "He reminds me of the pageant coordinator back in River Heights. What was her name—Twinkie?"

"Cupcake," I said glumly.

"Right. I knew it was some kind of dessert food."

I laughed, but I had a feeling Harrison was going to be even harder to please than Cupcake Hughes. And she had been impossible!

An hour later, though, I was feeling cheerful again. Bess had ordered me a Caesar salad with grilled shrimp from room service, and it was delicious. Harrison might have told me not to use so much dressing, but frankly I didn't care. I was happy with the way I looked, even if he wasn't.

"Guys, I think I'd better get some sleep," I said at last. "It's been a long day."

"So tomorrow we're going to check out Greenwich Village and SoHo, right?" Bess said, her eyes sparkling with excitement. Sitting cross-legged on her bed, she flipped through the packet of brochures she'd picked up from the hotel concierge. "There's so much to see! The designer stores . . . the funky downtown shops . . ."

". . . the Hudson River Park, the outdoor trapeze school by the river. . . ," George chimed in from the window seat, where she sat taking in the view of the river by night.

"Oooh, and we could take a Circle Line cruise around Manhattan Island to see the skyline!" Bess declared. "And the Statue of Liberty!"

I stood and picked up my high-heeled sandals, which I'd taken off as soon as we got into the room. "That sounds great, you guys, but don't forget I've got pageant work to do," I reminded them. "I don't have much free time. And I don't want to get on Harrison's bad side."

"Don't worry, George and I will help you keep your nose clean," Bess said.

I smiled at my friends. "'Night, you two."

I let myself out and walked down the plush, carpeted hall to the room Kelly and I were sharing. When I entered, she was already in bed, eyes closed, so I tried to be as quiet as I could.

I put on my pajamas, walked into the bathroom, and went through the presleep beauty routine Pretty Face recommended. I used their gentle daily cleanser to wash my face, then used a cotton pad to stroke toner over my skin. I moisturized with their nighttime revitalizing cream mousse, dabbing it on gently with my fingertips, then finished by patting some Essence of Dew Eye Soother around my eyes. Finally I was ready to brush my teeth.

I tossed the cotton pad at the garbage can, but missed. I bent to pick it up. That's when I noticed a smear of red on the white plastic garbage liner. It looked like . . . blood!

Frowning, I shook the edge of the can to shift the contents. A crumpled tissue rolled to one side and I spotted a small plastic bottle labeled TRANSPARENT NONDRYING STAGE BLOOD. It was empty but for a few drops.

I crouched there on my heels, trying to understand what I was seeing. Stage blood? Why was there an empty bottle of stage blood in our bathroom?

Suddenly I flashed back to Kelly's flushed face and furtive manner as she slipped back into the reception room after the animal-rights protesters were hauled away. The animal-rights protesters who'd been made up with gallons of stage blood.

Had Kelly had something to do with that protest? It seemed as though nothing else could explain the stage blood in the garbage can.

Why on earth would Kelly want to sabotage her own father's company?

SOHO TIME-OUT

I fell asleep with questions buzzing in my brain, and they were still there when I woke up the next morning.

Kelly was just finishing up in the shower. When she came out, I decided to see how she would react to a little subtle digging.

"So what did you think of the unscheduled entertainment at the reception?" I asked her.

Her cheeks turned pink. "I . . . I missed most of it. I was, um, in the ladies' room," she told me without looking at me. Taking the towel off her hair, she began to comb it out.

"Oh. Well, I thought your dad did a great job of calming the crowd down," I said. "But still, it was weird. I mean, Pretty Face wouldn't test their products on animals, would they?"

"No way," Kelly said without hesitation. "Those kids were dead wrong. My dad is always going on about how eco-friendly the company is. He says it's a central part of the branding. No, there's no way."

She finished combing her hair and went into the bathroom, where I heard the blow-dryer start up. I leaned back against my pillows, chewing on my lip. Okay, so it didn't seem likely that Kelly had been involved with the protest. Surely, if she had, she'd be trying to convince me that the protesters had been telling the truth. Right?

Unless she knew I was suspicious and was trying to throw me off the scent. . . .

I shook my head. No way would sweet, straightforward Kelly think like that.

Kelly walked back into the room. "So what did you do after the reception?" she asked. "Did you end up going out on the town?"

I climbed reluctantly out of bed. "Nope. We were too tired. I just hung out with Bess and George for a little while. How about you?"

"A few of the girls came back to the room for a bit. Oh, I hope you don't mind," she added, suddenly looking anxious. "I would have asked if it was okay with you, but I didn't know where you were."

"Of course I don't mind," I assured her. "So who was here?"

"Alanna, Piper, Crystal, and Juliet. We hung out and swapped pageant stories," Kelly told me. A wistful look crossed her face. "I know I sound like a dork, but it was really fun, just hanging out with the girls."

I felt a surge of sympathy. "It's one of the most fun things there is," I agreed. Kelly's dad was so ridiculously overprotective that Kelly basically had no friends back home. I'd seen that firsthand during the Miss Pretty Face River Heights pageant. I'd hung out at her house a couple of times, but it was hard to feel comfortable when her dad kept finding excuses to check up on us every ten minutes. And the few times I'd invited her to do something with me, he always had reasons why she couldn't go.

I caught sight of the clock. "Yikes!" I exclaimed. "If I don't get myself in gear, I'm going to be late for the morning workout!"

Kelly gave me a devilish grin. "Better you than me," she said. As the *former* Miss Pretty Face River Heights, she didn't have to do any of the pageant preparation. "Hmm. Maybe I'll go back to bed. Or order a big breakfast from room service."

"Don't rub it in," I retorted, grinning back at her.

I hurried into the bathroom and took a quick shower to wake myself up. After I dried my hair, I threw on my workout clothes, grabbed my white-soled sneakers, and headed down to the lobby and out the front doors. Harrison had told us the workout studio was a block and a half from the hotel. As I walked down the street, I glanced at the pageant schedule I'd snatched from my bag, searching for the address. Then I did a double take.

"The studio is at the corner of West Fourth and West Twelfth?" I muttered. How was that possible? Shouldn't those two streets run parallel to each other?

"Excuse me," I said, stopping a woman pushing a stroller down the street. I blinked as I noticed that the stroller held not a baby but a small, fat pug dog. The dog wore a hat and booties. It stared at me and yawned.

"Yes?" the woman said.

"Um . . ." I pulled my attention back to her. "I'm looking for the New York Fitness Studio, but I think there must be some mistake, because the directions I have say it's at the corner of West Fourth and West Twelfth streets." I laughed. "That's impossible, right?"

The woman looked at me with raised eyebrows. "I don't know why you'd say that," she snapped, as if I had just insulted her dog. Turning, she pointed down the street. "The corner of West Fourth and West Twelfth is two blocks south and two blocks east."

"Oh. Well, thanks," I said, mentally shaking my head. Greenwich Village was weird!

I hurried on and, five minutes later, was relieved to see the New York Fitness Studio banner waving from the side of a white-painted brick building. I ran up the stairs to the second-floor dance studio and slipped into place at the end of the line of contestants, intercepting a glare from Piper Depken. I was only two minutes late, which I thought was pretty good considering I'd still been in my pajamas half an hour before.

Harrison Hendrickson entered about thirty seconds after me, and without saying a single word, began walking up and down the line studying us.

"Good morning, ladies," he said after he'd given us all the once-over. He ran a hand over his perfectly combed silver hair. "I'm glad to see you're all here, properly dressed and on time. There's nothing more important for you, as representatives of Pretty Face, than to always be on time and looking your best." He stopped and peered at Raven's face. "I think you forgot to remove your makeup before you went to sleep last night," he said with that stiff smile. "Bad for the complexions, sweet pea."

Raven flushed. "I'm sorry, I was so tired I just fell asleep," she stammered, but Harrison held up a hand to silence her.

"No excuses," he said. "Just don't do it again.

"I'm going to go over the rules of conduct again, though I'm sure none of you young ladies would dream of breaching them," he went on, turning back to face the rest of us. "Miss Pretty Face, first and foremost, always has a pretty face and a natural look. She takes care of herself, and the way she looks reflects this. Miss Pretty Face is always well-spoken and polite. Miss Pretty Face is always punctual. Miss Pretty Face is always dressed appropriately for whatever occasion she is attending. Miss Pretty Face does not give unauthorized or unsupervised interviews or otherwise interact with the press. It goes without saying that Miss Pretty Face does not drink or take drugs of any kind. Miss Pretty Face . . ."

As he went on and on, I couldn't help tuning out. My stomach was growling, since I hadn't had time for breakfast. I hope the workout isn't too tough, I thought.

Two and a half hours later I practically crawled out of the studio, exhausted and frazzled. After the lecture Harrison had introduced us to Nadia, our Tae Bo coach, who'd led us in a grueling hour-long workout that included way too much kicking and punching for my liking. Then we'd done a half hour of concentrated abs, and finally Harrison called us all over and gave us personal evaluations. He'd seated himself behind a table at one side of the studio, a clipboard in front of him and a silver pen in his hand. We lined up to hear his verdicts one by one.

When it came to my turn, he said, "I noticed you came in late this morning."

"It was just two minutes," I said, startled.

"That's two minutes too many, sweet pea," he said, rapping my knuckles lightly with the silver pen. "Did you hear what I said in my opening remarks? Or maybe you don't think that punctuality is important?"

I was annoyed, but I kept my smile. "Of course I do, but it was only two minutes."

Harrison narrowed his eyes at me. "I see" was all he said. But suddenly I had the feeling that I had not made a good impression.

"You look worried about something," George said to me when I met her and Bess in the hotel lobby.

"Not worried, exactly," I said. "I just don't think I've gotten off on the right foot with Harrison Hendrickson. If there is a right foot with him."

"I don't think there is," Bess said. "He didn't strike me as a very nice man."

I shrugged. "Well, this pageant would be easier if he was a little less of a drill sergeant. But I'd rather think about something else for a while. Let's get out of here and check out the town!"

"Now you're speaking my language!" Bess cheered.

I changed into jeans and we trooped out to sightsee in New York City.

Our first stop was Magnolia Bakery, a famous Greenwich Village bakery on Bleecker Street, where we had delicious cupcakes with buttercream icing. Then we strolled over to Washington Square Park and watched some really good jugglers and musicians perform in the empty fountain in the middle of the park. From there we headed south into SoHo, land of Bess's dreams, where we window-shopped at one amazing store after another. My favorite was this weird little place, where you could buy anything from fossil dinosaur teeth to a full human skeleton. I picked up a shark tooth for Ned, my boyfriend back home. "Because nothing says I love you like the canine of a great white shark," George joked.

Of course Bess had to try on clothes in some of the designer boutiques, and George dragged us to a few electronics stores, while none of us could resist stopping in at a place that sold fancy bath and beauty products.

"Look, Nan, they've got the whole Pretty Face line!" Bess said excitedly.

I glanced over to where she was pointing. My eyes widened. There was a mob of women about three deep around the Pretty Face counter.

"Wow." Even George was impressed. "I guess Pretty Face must be doing something right. I mean, this is one of the most exclusive stores in the country."

"Oh my gosh," Bess whispered. She showed me the price sticker on a jar of Perfect Face. "I didn't realize it cost so much! Now I know why Perfect Face feels so fabulous—it must be made of liquid gold."

I counted the number of women around the Pretty Face counter and did some quick math in my head. I blinked. "If Perfect Face is selling this fast all over the country, they're really raking in the bucks," I said. "I had no idea the company was this successful."

"Does it make you feel rich?" George asked with a grin.

I laughed. "Not really, but I'll bet Kyle does. Come on, let's get out of here."

We headed further downtown and got on the Staten Island Ferry. We rode the huge orange ship out through New York Harbor, marveling at the dozens of tugboats, barges, tankers, cruise ships, sailboats, and more that dotted the water. New York was just as crowded by sea as it was by land!

By the time we got off the ferry at the southern tip of Manhattan, it was getting pretty late, and we hadn't eaten since the cupcakes at Magnolia Bakery. "I say we head back up to the neighborhood of our hotel and find someplace to eat dinner," I suggested. Pulling out my Manhattan subway map, I consulted it, trying hard not to be too obvious—until I realized that everyone else around me was doing the same thing. There were a lot of tourists in New York.

"If we take this red train, it should leave us pretty close to the hotel," I said after a minute of puzzling over the crazy tangle of colored stripes that represented the different subway lines. "At least, I hope so."

"Not to worry," George announced. "My PDA has GPS."

"'My PDA has GPS'?" Bess repeated with a shudder. "That sounds like some kind of horrible disease."

"My personal data assistant has a Global Positioning System," George translated, speaking slowly as if Bess were from a foreign country. "It means I can navigate if we get lost." She started walking. "So let's go!"

"Um, George?" I said.

She turned to look at me. "What's up?"

"The subway station is that way." I pointed in the opposite direction from where she'd been going.

George's cheeks turned pink. Bess smirked. "Some navigator," she remarked as we all headed underground.

When we came up out of the subway in the Village, my cell phone chimed, letting me know that I had a message. As we strolled down the street, I pressed it to my ear.

The message was from Anna Chavez. "Nancy, I got your number from your friend Kelly. There's something I'd really like to discuss with you," her low, lightly accented voice said. "It's . . . it's probably best if we talk away from the office. Can we meet tomorrow morning? There's a café across the street from where I work. They make excellent Colombian coffee. Could we meet there at eight o'clock?" She told me the address. "Call me back and let me know if you can make it." There was a pause. "And, please . . . don't say anything to anyone about this."

I flipped my phone shut, intrigued. "Well, that's interesting."

"What is?" George wanted to know.

I told Bess and George about the message. "She asked me not to tell anyone, but I assume you guys don't count," I added.

"Right, we're nobody," Bess said cheerfully.

"Speak for yourself," George retorted. "Well, aren't you going to call her back, Nan?"

"I was just about to." Opening my phone again, I found her number in "recent calls" and pressed Send. The phone rang a few times, then Anna's voice mail picked up.

"Hola, it's Anna. Leave a message," I heard, and then a beep.

"Anna, it's Nancy," I said. "Eight tomorrow is fine—I'll see you at the café. I'm looking forward to it!"

"What do you think it's about?" George asked me.

I shook my head. "I'm not sure. But I wonder if it has something to do with that protest last night. I saw Anna talking to Kyle and that security guy, Adam Bedrossian, afterwards, and she looked worried about something."

"Well, I say no mysteries until tomorrow. Tonight is for food and fun. Hey, this place looks good," Bess said, scanning the menu of a little Italian restaurant. "Mmm. Lobster ravioli!"

I put my phone away and Bess, George, and I trooped into the restaurant. We were served by a good-looking waiter with dark, tousled hair and chiseled cheekbones. "I bet he's an actor," Bess whispered as he walked away. "I read that all waiters and waitresses in New York are just waiting for their big acting break."

By the time we finished eating it was almost nine p.m. Bess and George really wanted to go out and explore New York's nightlife, but the long day and the grueling exercise class that morning were starting to catch up with me. "I've got to be up early, anyway," I said, stifling a yawn. "You guys go ahead. You can tell me all about it tomorrow."

The hotel was only three or four blocks away, and with the help of her GPS, George was able to point me in the right direction. I strolled back slowly, enjoying the bustle and liveliness of the Greenwich Village streets.

When I let myself into the room I shared with Kelly, she was curled up on the couch watching TV. "I'm trying to see if there's anything about Pretty Face on the news," she told me, not taking her eyes off the screen.

"Why, did something happen today?" I asked, my interest roused.

"Those protesters staged another crazy scene today, right outside the new office building downtown near Wall Street," Kelly said. "A couple of them chained themselves to the door, according to my dad. The police showed up and arrested them for trespassing, but by then a reporter from one of the local cable news programs had heard about it and showed up with a camera crew. Daddy was been on the phone with them all afternoon, trying to convince them not to run the story." She leaned back and stretched out her legs. "I think he must have succeeded, because the news is just about over and I haven't seen anything about it."

"That is so weird," I said. "I wonder why the protesters picked Pretty Face to target with their accusations? I mean, surely there are other cosmetics companies that really do animal testing. Why not go after them?"

"I don't get it," Kelly agreed, shaking her head. "It's just so unfair. I feel really bad for Daddy. I've never seen him so stressed out."

I sank down beside her on the couch. "I figured you'd be out on the town tonight," I told her. "After all, trips to New York City don't happen every day."

She sighed. "I was dying to go out, but Daddy didn't want me to. He worries about me getting mugged or something. I tried to tell him New York is safer than most big cities these days, but he didn't buy it." She looked seriously bummed out.

"Well, maybe we can do something together tomorrow night," I suggested. "Do you think your dad would be okay with that? If it helps, tell him I know some martial arts. And George is really tough." I grinned. "We'll protect you, I promise."

To my surprise Kelly flushed and turned her face away. "Oh, uh—that's okay," she stammered. "I—I don't want to argue with Daddy when he's so stressed already."

"There's no harm in asking—," I began, but she cut me off.

"No! I mean, don't worry about me. I'll find something to do, I'm sure."

Jumping up, she hurried into the bathroom and shut the door, leaving me sitting there, wondering.

One thing was for sure: Kelly was hiding something. It was painfully obvious—the girl was totally unused to keeping secrets. But it was obvious she was keeping one now.

The question was, did it have anything to do with Pretty Face and the protesters? Because when I put Kelly's strange behavior together with Anna's intriguing phone call, I was definitely getting a familiar feeling: I had another mystery on my hands.

VANISHING ACT

I got up at seven the next morning. I didn't want to be late for Anna, plus I wanted to go over the order of the day's events. Much as I hated to admit it, I was intimidated by Harrison Hendrickson. I didn't want to get on his bad side any more than I already was.

Before I went out, I studied my schedule. I had a makeup consultation here at the hotel with someone named Vita at 9:45, a toning session at New York Fitness at eleven, and talent coaching at noon. Then nothing until a party with press at some club in the evening. Well, as long as I kept an eye on the clock during my meeting with Anna, I would be fine.

I headed out and, with the help of my trusty

subway map, got myself up to west Midtown in twenty minutes. I found Café al Gusto easily, just two blocks from the subway stop. Not bad, I thought. I'm getting pretty good at navigating around New York!

I was a few minutes early, so I wasn't surprised to see that Anna hadn't arrived at the café yet. I sat down inside, at a table near the back. Since, according to Anna, the Pretty Face offices were across the street, I thought it would be best if we sat someplace where she wasn't too noticeable.

I ordered a mocha latte and flipped through my New York City guidebook while I waited. There was a section on the early history of the city, and I got caught up in reading it. When I glanced at my watch, I was surprised to see that it was already 8:20. Anna was nowhere in sight. Was she running late? Or had I somehow ended up in the wrong place?

I called her on my cell phone, but her voice mail came on immediately, which told me that wherever Anna was, her phone was turned off.

"Anna, it's Nancy," I said after the beep. "I'm at Café al Gusto as we arranged, but it's eight twenty and you're not here. Did I get the time or place wrong? Please call me. Thanks."

I hung up and went back to my reading, figuring she'd either show up or call me in the next few minutes.

Fifteen minutes later, though, Anna still hadn't called. What's more, the waitress was starting to look annoyed with me, since the café was full and I was hogging a table. To make her happy, I ordered a toasted bagel and another latte. Then I dialed Anna's number one more time.

Once again the phone sent me straight to voice mail. "Anna, it's Nancy again," I said. "I'm starting to get worried about you. Please call me back as soon as you get this message." I repeated my phone number, even though I figured she already had it since she'd called me before, and hung up.

My bagel and second latte arrived. By now I was too antsy to read anymore. I nibbled at my breakfast, wondering what could have gone wrong. Had Anna forgotten about our meeting? Had she said eight at *night*? No, that definitely wasn't it—she'd specifically mentioned breakfast.

I called Information and got the address of Pretty Face's corporate headquarters. The address told me that it was, in fact, right across the street from where I was. I was definitely in the right place.

So where, then, was Anna?

At 9:10 I decided it was pointless to wait any longer. It was clear that Anna wasn't coming. And I was determined to be five minutes early for my makeup consultation, just to prove to Harrison that I could be.

I called the Pretty Face offices and left a message on Anna's work phone, telling her that if she wanted to talk to me she should call my cell this afternoon. Then I hurried back to the subway. A train was just coming into the station as I got there, so I swiped my card, raced through the turnstile, and jumped on.

It wasn't until fifteen minutes had gone by that I realized I was on the train going *up*town, not downtown. . . .

"Oh, no!" I gasped out loud.

The guy in the seat next to me, a big, hulking man in baggy clothes, turned to look at me. "Is something wrong, Miss?" he rumbled politely.

"I'm going the wrong way," I moaned. "I'm supposed to be in Greenwich Village in fifteen minutes."

The guy peered out at the station we were pulling into. "I think you're going to be late," he told me sympathetically.

"Me, too," I agreed with a sinking heart.

"Just get off the train here, cross over to the

downtown side at the end of the platform, and wait for the next train," he advised. Then he patted my shoulder. "Relax. Being late isn't the end of the world."

"Thanks," I told him, smiling over my shoulder as I jumped out. He was really nice. But unfortunately for me, being late might as well be the end of the world. At least, as far as Harrison Hendrickson was concerned.

The next downtown train arrived five minutes later. I stepped onboard and willed it to go faster, faster. But it crept along the subway tunnel, stopping once or twice for minutes at a time. By the time we pulled into my stop in Greenwich Village, my nerves were completely jangled. I ran up the stairs out of the station and careened down the street. A block later I realized I was heading the wrong direction—again. "Stupid, confusing New York City!" I muttered under my breath as I ran.

I rushed into the Horatio Hotel lobby at 9:57, out of breath and sweaty—and cannoned straight into someone who was walking in the opposite direction. To my horror, it was Harrison Hendrickson.

He staggered backward, caught himself, and gave me a frosty look. "You are not conducting yourself the way we expect Miss Pretty Face to conduct herself," he said. There was no smile, fake or otherwise, this time.

"I'm sorry," I gasped. "Got on the wrong train ... went uptown by mistake. . . ."

"Not interested," he snapped. "I have to tell you, sweet pea, I don't like the pattern I'm seeing with you."

"But I—"

"Ah, ah, ah!" He held up his hand in his trademark silencing gesture. "I told you, not interested in your excuses. All I care about is your actions. Now get on up to suite five-oh-two for your makeup consultation."

Before I could say anything else, he swept off, leaving me behind.

It wasn't until later that afternoon that I was able to even think about Anna Chavez again. After the makeup consultation, there had been another incredibly exhausting workout—who knew yoga could be so hard?—and then individual talent coaching sessions. My talent coach, a bouncy, cheerful woman named Clarice, had listened to me sing with a gradually fading smile. When I was done, she said, "That was very . . . nice. But—well, I'm just not sure 'My Heart Will Go On' is the right song for you, dear. Perhaps something a little more upbeat?"

I winced. Was I really that bad? "It's the only song I know well enough to perform."

She gave a shake of her head. "Well, we'll just have to work with what we've got, then, won't we?"

My head was starting to throb. "I guess so," I said glumly.

"Good. Now, place your hand on your diaphragm like *this*," Clarice said. "Take a deep breath, but don't allow your upper chest to inflate. Yes. Now—unvoiced lip trill. *Brrrrrrrrrr!*"

"*Brrrrrrrrrr!*" I echoed obediently.

"*Brrrrrrrr!*" she said again with a stern look.

"*Brrrrrrr!*" I tried again.

"Now on an octave. *BrrrrRRRRRrrrr.*"

"*BrrrRRRrrr!*" I sang.

"Yes! That's *it*!" Clarice cried, clapping her hands together. I had no idea what "it" was, but I was glad to be doing something right for once today.

We worked together for an hour, and at the end of it Clarice seemed happy with my progress. I was glad of that, but even more, I was starving.

I called Bess and George's room to see if they were around. They weren't. And neither was Kelly in our room. I went down to the hotel restaurant, ate an omelet and a salad, and bought some aspirin in a nearby drugstore for the headache I still had. Finally I thought to check my messages and found a text from Bess telling me that she and George had gone to get tickets for the two o'clock matinee of some new Broadway show and that I should come meet them. "We'll wait outside the theater until one-thirty," she wrote.

I checked my watch. It was quarter to two. "Great," I grumbled.

That was when I remembered Anna. It seemed so strange that she still hadn't called me. Since I didn't have anything else to do, I decided to take a trip up to the Pretty Face offices and see if she was there.

Of course the subways worked perfectly now that I wasn't in a rush, and fifteen minutes later I was asking the receptionist to buzz Anna for me. I wasn't entirely surprised when she didn't pick up her phone.

"I haven't seen her today," the receptionist told me, "but maybe I just missed her. The company has grown so much over the last few months, I can't keep track of all the faces anymore. Let me try another number. What's your name, please?"

"Nancy Drew. I'm Miss Pretty Face River Heights," I told her. "We had an appointment."

She spoke into the phone. "It's Lisa. Is Anna in today? No, I thought not. There's someone here who had an appointment with her." She paused. "Okay, great."

She hung up. "Anna isn't here today," she told me. "But her lab mate is on his way out. There he is now."

I turned around and saw a young man with short black hair and wire-rimmed glasses striding toward me. "I'm Marty Anders," he said. "Come on back to the lab."

"Anna had a family emergency," he went on as I followed him down the hall. "Is there something I can help you with?"

"A family emergency?" I repeated. "Is it her brother?"

"I'm not sure. I got an e-mail from her, sent early this morning. She had to fly back home to Venezuela suddenly. She said she'd be in touch in a couple of days."

"Venezuela?" I said, startled. I was pretty sure Anna had told me she didn't have any family left in Venezuela.

He shrugged. "That's what the e-mail said."

"Do you mind if I have a look at it?" I asked.

Marty gave me a sharp sidelong glance. "You don't believe me?"

"No, no, it's nothing like that," I said quickly. "I just—I'm surprised, that's all. Wondering if she said anything else."

"She didn't," he told me. "But if you want to see it, be my guest." We entered a largish room with a biochemistry lab setup. Two doors on either side led to small offices, one of which Marty led me to. He clicked his computer mouse a few times and an e-mail popped up. Reading it, I could see that it had been sent from Anna's work Web-mail address. It was short and to the point. "I have to go to Venezuela for a family emergency. I will be in touch soon."

"And that's all she wrote," Marty added. "I guess we'll hear from her when she's able. Now, is there something *I* can help you with?"

"No, I don't think so. My appointment with Anna was about something personal," I said, thinking hard. "Can I just ask you one thing? Did you hear about the animal-rights protesters that crashed the Miss Pretty Face reception two nights ago?"

"Yeah, that was the craziest thing," Marty said, sinking down onto a lab chair. "I worked in product testing up until a few months ago, and believe me when I say Pretty Face does not test on animals. I'm the one who had to run the protocols on human volunteers. But really, we did most of our testing by computer simulation."

"Could they have changed their methods recently?" I asked. "I mean, since you stopped working in that area?"

"I don't see why they would," Marty told me. He leaned back and laced his fingers behind his head. "The computer simulations and human tests give more accurate information than animal tests ever will. Makes sense—why should a rabbit's eyes react to makeup the same way a human's eyes do? We're different species. Anyway, the hard part about human testing and computer simulation is actually getting it up and running. Pretty Face did all that years ago. So there's no point in them switching methods now. They're using the best science, and it's also the easiest for them."

"I see." I stood there, frowning as I thought things over.

I still had no real reason to believe there was something sinister going on, but my gut was starting to say that there was. True, I didn't know Anna well, but she hadn't struck me as the type of person who would make an appointment and then just not show up without even a phone call. And she *had* said she had no family in Venezuela, so what was this "trip home" all about? And finally, why were the protesters targeting Pretty Face when it seemed so clear that there wasn't a scrap of truth in their accusations?

I thanked Marty and headed back to the Horatio. To my surprise, Bess and George were there.

"The only tickets we could get were for some kids' play featuring a talking bat," George explained. "We figured we'd skip it."

"Well, I'm sorry you didn't find a good show, but I'm glad you're here," I told her. "I need your computer help."

I filled my friends in about Anna's vanishing act as we went up to their room. "I need to track down her brother," I said. "But all I know is that he was born in Venezuela, he's a chemist at a Texas oil company, and his last name is Chavez."

"That's it?" Bess sounded incredulous. "Nancy, do you have any idea how many people there probably are in Texas named Chavez? You'll never find him!"

"Calm down," George said, waving a hand. "Let me do some searches."

She turned on her computer, which of course

was immediately wirelessly connected to the Internet, and started typing away at her various search engines.

"You said he's a chemist?" she called a few moments later.

"Right."

"Okay. Just checking." George resumed typing.

"Hmm. *Nació en* means 'born in' in Spanish, right?" she called after five or ten minutes more.

"I think so," I replied.

"Got it."

Bess handed me a bottle of water from the minibar. "Get comfortable. This will take hours," she advised. "Want to watch a movie on pay-per-view?"

"Found him," George announced.

"*Already?*" Bess and I said at the same time.

George shrugged, grinning. "Wasn't so hard. I had to break through the security on a couple of the oil company Web sites to get their employee directories, but that stuff's usually fairly low-level. Then I took all the Chavezes that came out of those searches and checked their college degrees. There were only two with degrees in chemistry. After that I just had to figure out which one was born in Venezuela. No problem."

"Right. Simple," I said with a snort. "George,

has anyone ever told you you're a genius?"

"Not often enough," she said smugly.

"So can your genius take you one step further and find his office phone number for me?" I asked.

"Right here." She pointed to her computer screen. "I'm a full-service operation."

I dialed the number on the screen. After two rings a man answered. "Otilio Chavez."

"Mr. Chavez, my name is Nancy Drew. I'm a friend of your sister, Anna," I said.

"Yes?" The man's voice sounded puzzled and a bit alarmed. "Is something wrong?"

"Well, sir, that's what I was hoping you'd tell me," I explained. "Anna sent an e-mail saying she had a family emergency and was flying home to Venezuela. I just wanted to find out if everything was all right."

"That doesn't make any sense," Mr. Chavez said. "We don't have family in Venezuela. Are you sure that's what she said?"

"I'm sure," I said. The bad feeling in my gut was getting stronger. "So I assume you haven't heard from her."

"Not since last weekend," Mr. Chavez said. "We talked on the phone on Sunday. Everything seemed fine. And I certainly don't know about any family emergency. Look, what is going on? Who am I speaking with, anyway?"

"Mr. Chavez, I'm a friend of Anna's. I met her recently at a Pretty Face event. She called me yesterday to say she wanted to talk to me about something. But she never showed up for our meeting."

"I don't understand," he said. "Should I call the police?"

"I don't think there's anything they can do," I told him. "If she is missing, she's been gone less than a full day, and that's not long enough to start an investigation." I bit my lip. "I'd like to help. If you give me her address, I can go over there and see if there's any more information I can pick up about where she is."

"Well . . ." I could hear his hesitation. "All right. It seems strange, since I don't even know you, but . . . I don't know what else to do. Listen, will you please call me and tell me what you find out?"

"I will," I promised.

Grabbing a pen, I scribbled down the address he gave me. Then I hung up and used an online map site to show me how to get there. Anna's place turned out to be quite close to the hotel.

"Anyone up for a brief excursion?" I asked.

"You know we are," Bess told me. She grabbed her bag. "Let's go."

We hurried through the narrow, cobblestone streets of the far West Village. Ten minutes later we stood in front of Anna's building, a smallish four-story brick structure on a tree-lined street. A grizzled, elderly man in blue work pants was hosing down the sidewalk in front of the building. "Can I help you ladies?" he asked as he noticed us hesitating on the stoop. "I'm the super of this building."

"We're friends of Anna Chavez in 4B," I told him. "She was supposed to meet us earlier today and she never showed up. She's not answering her phone, either. We just wanted to make sure she was okay."

He frowned. "Anna? Buzz her."

I pressed the buzzer for 4B. No one answered the intercom.

"Did you see her leave this morning, by any chance?" I asked the super.

"Nope." He shrugged. "I saw her come in last night, around ten, ten thirty. But today, I didn't see her."

I took a deep breath. "Look, I know this is asking a lot, but would you mind going up there with us and opening her door? I just want to make sure she's not sick or passed out or something in there."

His eyes narrowed. "You sure this isn't some kind of scam? You're not just trying to get into her apartment and steal stuff?"

"I swear it's not a scam," I said. "Anyway, you'll be with us the whole time. You can keep an eye on us."

He glared at me, then shifted his gaze to Bess and George. We all did our best to look as trustworthy as possible.

After a moment he gave a curt nod. "Okay. Anna's a good girl. I don't like to think of anything bad happening to her. You come up with me. But no touching anything, you got it?"

I nodded, then waited impatiently while he went to his own apartment to get Anna's spare key. He led us up the four flights of stairs to her door. "Anna?" he called as he unlocked it. "Anna, you here?"

No answer.

Her place was small but light-filled, airy, and exquisitely neat. Tropical plants flourished in the windows, and the walls were covered with photographs of exotic flowers and animals.

A plaintive mewing made me look down. A

small tortoiseshell cat was winding around my legs. As soon as I took a step toward the kitchen, it scampered ahead of me, then turned to look back expectantly.

"That cat is hungry," George observed.

I stepped into the kitchen and looked around. The sink had one or two dirty dishes in it that looked as if they'd been there at least a day, judging from the crust of dried food on the rim of the bowl. That seemed out of place, given how neat the place was overall. I noticed, too, that the cat's food bowl was empty and its water dish dry. It mewed again.

"That's funny," the super said. "That cat don't eat much. Anna always pays me to feed it when she goes away, and it never empties the bowl. She must not have fed it in a while."

"She didn't tell you she was going away today, did she?" I asked.

"Nope."

I looked up and met Bess's and George's gazes. They both had the same worried look I knew must have been on my own face. Surely Anna would never go away and leave her cat uncared for, even if there was some kind of family emergency. Put that together with the dirty dishes in the sink and the appointment she had never shown up for . . .

There was no hard evidence, but the feeling in my gut had grown to a near certainty.

Something had happened to Anna Chavez. Something bad.

HUNTING FOR CLUES

We thanked Anna's super and left the building as quickly as we could. "What should we do?" Bess asked as we hurried back toward the hotel. "Shouldn't we call the police?"

I shook my head. "Like I told Anna's brother, there really isn't anything the police could do. They won't declare a person officially missing and open an investigation until no one's seen the person for something like two full days. And it's not like there are any signs of violence in Anna's apartment or anything."

"So we're on our own," George said.

"For now," I agreed.

Back at the hotel, we returned to Bess and

George's room. I didn't want Kelly to overhear what we were about to discuss—especially since I was worried that she might be involved in some way.

"Okay," I said when we were all sitting down. "Let's figure out what we know so far."

"Do we know anything at all?" Bess asked doubtfully.

"Well, we know Anna was troubled by something," George pointed out. "Troubled enough to call Nancy about it."

"And it seems reasonable to think it had something to do with the protest at the reception," I added. "After all, I saw her having an argument or something with Kyle McMahon right after the protest. And she called me the next day."

"I still can't believe the protesters could be right about Pretty Face," Bess objected. "I mean, their whole reputation is built on the fact that they don't do animal testing! If it turns out that's a lie, they're finished!"

"Pretty good reason to want to keep it a secret, isn't it?" I said grimly.

Bess's eyes widened. "You think Kyle McMahon is behind her disappearance? You think she was going to blow the whistle and he made sure she couldn't?"

"I think it's a good place to start," I said.

"Couldn't it be something else, though?" George argued. "I mean, Pretty Face must have competitors, other companies who are trying to sell to the same market. Maybe someone in one of the rival companies set up the protests to smear Pretty Face."

"And Anna found out about it and the people at the rival company had to keep her from spilling the beans," I finished. "Yeah, that's a possibility too, George. Good thinking. Either way, there are a few things we need to investigate. I know you two are here on vacation, but I'm going to need a lot of help on this."

"You know we're with you," Bess said. "Finding Anna is more important than our vacation."

"What she said," George chimed in.

I smiled at my two best friends. Where would I be without them?

"Okay," I said, grabbing a pen and a pad of Horatio Hotel notepaper from the desk. Scribbling stuff down helps me think. "Let's break down our tasks.

"First, I need to trace Anna's movements as much as I can to get a better idea of exactly when and where she disappeared."

"You don't think she's . . . well . . . you don't

think whoever kidnapped her did something bad to her, do you?" Bess asked hesitantly.

I bit my lip. I'd been wondering the same thing.

"Well, the e-mail that was sent out to cover her disappearance did say she'd be in touch in a few days," I pointed out. "Let's hope that means that whoever took her plans to release her at some point."

"I wonder if I could figure out where that e-mail really came from," George murmured.

"You read my mind. That was the next thing I was going to suggest," I said, grinning. "If I can get you access to Kyle McMahon's computer, could you get into his e-mail and see whether or not he's the one who sent that message?"

"Not a problem," George declared. "Chances are, all I have to do is figure out his password."

"Great." I wrote that task down. "Now, the next thing on my list is for you, Bess," I went on.

"Good, I was starting to feel left out," she said.

"I need you to hang out with Kelly. You're trying to find out two things. First, see if you can get any details from her on what her father was doing between . . ." I checked the call log on my cell phone to see what time Anna's call had come in. "Between six fifty p.m. yesterday and seven thirty this morning. That's what time the e-mail was sent, so whatever happened to Anna happened somewhere in that time period.

"Second, I want you to see if you can figure out what Kelly's secret is. I know she has one, and I think it might have something to do with those protesters." I'd already told Bess and George about the tube of stage blood in the trash can. "I invited her to hang out with us tonight, and she started acting funny, which makes me think she has some plans of her own that she doesn't want me to know about. But you might have better luck than me. It seems as though, ever since she found out I'm a detective, she hasn't really trusted me all the way. See if you can get her to tell you anything."

"On it," Bess said, nodding.

"I also think we should try to find one of the protesters and see if we can get them to tell us where they're getting their information," I said, making a few more notes. "George, if I get you the protesters' names, can you make some calls and see what you can find out?"

George shrugged. "Not a problem. But what are you going to be doing?"

"I'm going up to the Pretty Face offices to see if I can get into Anna's office. There might be some clues in there."

First I made a quick phone call to one of my more useful contacts, Officer Ellen Johansen, of the River Heights Police Department. We get along really well and, whenever we can, we help each other out on cases. She's one of the few police officers in River Heights who doesn't resent me for solving more mysteries than they do.

I asked Officer Johansen to call a friend in the New York City Police Department and have them give her the contact information for any protesters who'd been arrested yesterday. I gave her George's number so that she could pass the info to George as soon as she got it.

"Okay," I said at last, clapping my hands together. "Let's hope that'll bring us some clues." I checked my watch and saw that it was already nearly five o'clock in the afternoon. "Yikes! I'd better get going. I'll meet you guys back here at six fifteen."

Once more I got on the subway and headed uptown. I hadn't quite figured out how I would persuade the receptionist to let me into Anna's office, but as I came into the building I spotted Anna's lab mate, Marty Anders, hurrying out. He must be leaving for the day. Maybe I can use that.

Upstairs, I saw that the receptionist was tidying up her desk and getting ready to go. "I'm sorry to bother you," I said, "but I left my day planner in the lab. Could you call Mr. Anders for me?"

"He's already gone for the day," she said.

I bit my lip. "Can I just quickly go back there? I know exactly where I left it."

The receptionist looked doubtful. "I'm not supposed to let anyone back without an escort. But I've got to get going—my boyfriend is waiting downstairs for me."

Perfect! "I promise I'll go straight to the lab— I remember how to get there," I said. "Please, I hate to ask you to bend the rules, but I really need my day planner."

The receptionist hesitated. Then she nodded. "Okay, I guess you're technically part of the company, since you're a Miss Pretty Face." She pointed toward the door. "Go ahead. I'll buzz you through. Just don't get me in trouble, okay?"

"I'll be out in a flash," I promised. "Thanks!"

She buzzed me through the security door and I hurried back to the lab. Anna's office was the one across the lab from Marty's, I guessed. The door was closed and through the frosted glass I could see that there were no lights on. I slipped inside, leaving it dark and closing the door again so that no one would notice me if they happened by, and turned on the computer.

While I waited for it to boot up, I glanced quickly over the surface of Anna's desk. Almost at once, I realized with a zing of excitement that someone else had been there before me. I mean, Anna was a neat person, but this desk was beyond neat. There was nothing on the wooden surface except a blank pad of paper. The in-tray was empty. Opening the file drawer, I saw that it had been emptied as well.

I turned back to the computer. "ENTER USER ID AND PASSWORD" was blinking at me from the middle of a blue screen. I groaned softly. "George, where are you when I need you?" I muttered. How was I ever going to figure out Anna's user ID and password?

I decided to tackle that after I searched the rest of Anna's desk drawers. Maybe the password was written down somewhere.

The other desk drawers appeared to hold nothing but a few boxes of paper clips and staples and some spare pens. Just to be thorough, I ran my fingers over the insides of each drawer.

Hey! "What's this?" I said out loud. Something

was taped to the underside of the drawer above the one I had opened. It felt like a piece of paper. Heart beating faster, I worked my fingertips under the tape and gently peeled it away.

I pulled out a square of glossy paper that had been folded in quarters. I was about to unfold it when I heard something that made the hairs on the back of my neck rise.

It was the click of Anna's office door, opening.

And then a deep, rumbling voice said, "Just what do you think you're doing?"

BREAKING AND ENTERING

jumped up and spun around. Standing behind me was the one person in the world I didn't think I could bluff—Adam Bedrossian, the head of corporate security for Pretty Face cosmetics.

Still, I had to try. "Wow," I said, giving him a big smile. "You startled me!" I spoke as casually as I could with my heart racing about a million beats a minute. "I was just looking for my day planner. I came up here this afternoon to talk to Anna and I think I left it somewhere in her office."

Adam folded his brawny arms. "Anna wasn't here today," he said, his eyes narrowing. "In fact, she's gone out of town for a while."

"I know," I said. "I talked to her lab mate, Marty. He brought me back here. I think that's when I left it behind." As far as Adam would be able to check, everything I had said so far was the truth. Unless, of course, he decided to search me and found my day planner in my purse. But I hoped he wouldn't go that far.

"You think you left your day planner in one of Anna's desk drawers?" Adam drawled, raising his eyebrows. "That seems . . . odd."

I forced a laugh. "No, of course not. But I thought if one of the cleaning staff had found it on her desk, they might have put it into one of the drawers. You know, for safekeeping."

"Smart thinking," Adam commented dryly. I had a feeling he wasn't talking about the office cleaning staff. In fact, I strongly suspected he didn't believe a word I was saying.

Abruptly he unfolded his arms and gestured toward the lab door. "I take it you didn't find it."

"Not yet," I said.

"Well." He smiled a humorless smile at me. "I think we can both agree that you're not going to find it here. So how about if I walk you to the elevator, and you get back to the beauty pageant."

"Sure, thanks," I said. There was no other response I could think of.

"It's a good thing I found you here," Adam told me as we walked down the empty, carpeted corridor. "I noticed Anna's computer was on. You know, we take our corporate security very, very seriously, Miss Drew. Our trade secrets are very valuable. If someone had found you, say, looking through Anna's computer files, I don't know that I would have been able to clear up any misunderstandings about what you were up to."

"Uh—right," I said, not sure where he was going with this.

"Trouble of that kind would probably get a girl kicked out of the Miss Pretty Face pageant," he went on, as if he were simply thinking aloud.

"Oh, I see what you mean," I said, my hackles rising as I realized what he was doing. He was threatening me! "I guess it's lucky for me that I *wasn't* looking through Anna's computer. I was just looking for my day planner." Of course, I would have looked through Anna's computer if I'd had the chance, but I hadn't, so . . .

"Lucky indeed," Adam agreed with a bland smile. We reached the elevator and he pressed the Down button. In less than ten seconds the doors swished open. "Well, have a nice evening, Miss Drew. Looking forward to seeing you onstage at the pageant." *And not before that,* he didn't have to add.

"Thanks for all your help," I said, giving him an equally fake smile and a little wave. "See you later."

A few minutes later I was back on the subway and heading downtown for what seemed like the millionth time that day. It was crowded with rush-hour traffic, so I had to stand. I stood there, clutching a pole and willing my pulse to slow down. That had been close—too close. I'd have to be extracareful from here on in. With Adam Bedrossian around, I couldn't afford to make any mistakes.

I considered the possibility that he might have some connection to Anna's disappearance. If he did, I knew there was no way I'd find out anything from talking to him. Adam Bedrossian was a pro and would never give anything away by accident.

If I was right about Kyle McMahon being behind Anna's disappearance, it was possible Adam was working with him. Still, I decided it made the most sense to investigate Kyle, not Adam. Kyle was Adam's boss, after all, so if they were working together, Kyle was probably the one giving the orders. Besides, I had a feeling it was going to be much easier to find out about him than it would be to find out about the security chief.

With a start I remembered the bit of paper I'd found taped inside Anna's desk. I pulled it out from the waistband of my jeans, where I'd quickly stuffed it before I turned around to face Adam.

I unfolded it. It was a page that had been torn from what seemed to be some kind of science or nature magazine. It had a photo of a small, brilliantly colored frog sitting on some kind of jungle leaf. Unfortunately, I couldn't make out much more than that because the entire article was written in Spanish. I ran my eyes over it, but the only words I could make out were *la rana* ("frog") and *venenosa*, which I guessed meant "venomous." I also saw the phrase *"la selva tropical Venezolana"* a couple of times. I vaguely remembered from Spanish class that *selva* was Spanish for "jungle." Venezuelan tropical jungle?

Why would Anna have taped part of an article about venomous frogs to the inside of her desk? As I stared at the page, trying to make out more of what it said, I noticed the date of the publication. The article had come out more than two years ago. So it wasn't even current!

I wrinkled my forehead. It didn't make any sense. What was so supersecret in an old article about a Venezuelan rain-forest frog?

Well, maybe if a Spanish speaker read the whole page, they could tell me what I was missing. My boyfriend Ned could probably help with that. He had a couple of friends at college who were Spanish majors. I could fax it to him and ask for a quick translation.

The subway arrived at my stop and I got off. By now I knew the way so well I didn't even have to pause and figure out where I was. I walked down the street toward the Horatio, dialing my cell phone.

Ned didn't answer his phone, so I left a message asking him to call me as soon as he could and to leave me a number where I could fax to him.

As I entered the hotel, I saw Harrison Hendrickson making a beeline for me, his face stormy. Oh, no, I thought, my stomach clenching. What have I done now?

"I just had a phone call about you," he said, not even bothering to say hello. "From the security director at Pretty Face. I understand you were caught wandering around the office after hours, unescorted."

So Adam Bedrossian had ratted me out. What a jerk!

"You are skating on *very* thin ice," Harrison said coldly. I noticed that he had stopped calling me "sweet pea," and although it had bugged me before, now I kind of wished I could hear it again. "I would have thought that, after what happened this morning, you would have started taking this pageant more seriously, but apparently not. Well, I'm putting you on notice. One more of your . . . lapses and you are out of this contest and the runner-up takes your place. Do you understand?"

"I—" was all I got out.

"Good," Harrison said curtly, and stalked away.

Feeling wilted and deflated, I headed for the bank of house phones. First I called Kyle McMahon's room and made sure that he wasn't there. Then I called up to Bess and George's room.

"You sound wiped out," George told me after we'd said hello. "Are you okay?"

"Yeah. I just got yelled at again by Harrison, but I've got more important things to worry about than the pageant wrangler." I looked around to be sure no one was within earshot. "Can you meet me at Kyle McMahon's room, four-oh-nine, in five minutes? It's time for that little job I asked for your help with."

"On my way," George said. We hung up.

I ran up to my own room, hoping that Kelly would be out too so I wouldn't have to hide what I was doing—which was grabbing my lock-pick set so that I could break into her father's room.

Fortunately the room was empty. I spent a brief moment wondering if Bess had learned anything useful about Kelly. Then I grabbed my tools and hurried down to 409, where George was waiting, looking nervous. The corridor was empty as far as I could see. "Tell me if you see or hear anyone coming," I instructed her, and set to work.

It took a few minutes for me to pick the lock. Hotel room doors are almost always high-tech, with electronic locks that have to be opened with a computerized key card. Luckily criminal technology had kept up with the times, and my tools were able to do the job.

The door light flashed green and I turned the knob. "We're in," I murmured, and slipped inside. George was right behind me.

"Whew! My heart is racing," she said with a shaky laugh. "We just committed a crime!"

"It's only a crime in the technical sense," I pointed out. "We're not here to steal anything, we're trying to solve a mystery and find a missing person."

"Somehow I doubt the judge at our trial is going to accept that as a defense," George retorted. She put a hand to her chest. "Okay, it's slowing down now. How do you stay so calm, Nan?"

I grinned. "Guess I'm just an outlaw at heart."

George had moved past me and was glancing around the room. "Um, I hate to say this, but I think the first mystery we need to solve is, how can I hack into Kyle McMahon's computer when it doesn't seem to be here?"

I groaned. "Oh, no!" Kyle must have his laptop with him wherever he is. I'd counted on him leaving it in the room, since he could access his e-mail and do lots of other things with his PDA.

"Looks like we broke in for nothing," George said. "What should we—"

She froze in the middle of her sentence, her eyes widening in horror. So did mine. We'd both heard the same sound.

The sound of the electronic lock on the room door clicking open.

Someone was about to walk into the room.

And we were about to get caught!

TRAPPED!

There was no way to explain our presence in Kyle McMahon's room. Somehow, I had the feeling "Whoops, we thought this was our room!" just wouldn't cut it.

I dug an elbow into George's ribs and pointed to the bed. She nodded and we both dove for the carpet. We wriggled our way under the bed on our bellies, like commandos. There was a terrible moment when my jeans pocket snagged on something sticking out of the bed frame, but then I heard a little rip and I was free. I slid forward another few inches and pulled my feet in under the dust ruffle.

Not a second too soon! I was facing in the direction of the door, and I saw the triangle of light from the hallway fall on the carpet as the door opened. I also heard Kyle McMahon's voice as he entered the room.

"I don't understand why you're bringing this problem to me, Carole," he was saying, apparently talking on his phone. There was an edge in his voice I hadn't heard before. "Production is your department, not mine. If the stuff hasn't arrived, get on the phone and find out where it is. I don't want excuses, I want product in the stores! We've got numbers we have to hit, or we're both in trouble."

I watched his feet move over to the desk. There was a gentle thud; he must have been putting stuff down on the desktop. Maybe his laptop? A lot of good that would do George and me, trapped under the bed!

"Look, this conversation is a waste of my time. And between the pageant and the new offices downtown, not to mention my regular workload, time is not something I have to waste right now. As we discussed in this morning's staff meeting." Kyle exhaled heavily. "Just fix it, Carole. Do whatever you have to do. Perfect Face is our biggest hit ever, and we cannot mess it up. Not acceptable. I don't care if you have to fly to Caracas and pick the stuff up yourself—just get it. All right?"

Under the bed, George and I looked at each other. Caracas? That was a city in Venezuela—where Anna was supposed to have gone. Was there a connection there?

"Right," Kyle said into the phone. "No, not tonight—I've got a dinner at seven and the Club Mirador party after that. Send me an e-mail and let me know. Right. Talk to you tomorrow."

After he hung up, he sighed again and walked toward the bathroom. The light went on and we heard water running in the sink. That would have been the perfect time for us to make our escape. But unfortunately the bathroom was right between us and the room door, and there was no way to get past it without being spotted. So we stayed put.

The water shut off and Kyle walked back into the bedroom. I heard the beep of his cell phone as he punched in a number. "Hi, Marsha, it's Kyle. Could you messenger six more press packets to the hotel? I need them here in an hour. And call Adam and let him know that I want to talk to him at ten. No, ten tonight, not tomorrow morning."

Wow, the guy never stopped working!

Kyle's feet stopped by the bed and I heard him sit down. The bottom of the bed sagged a little under his weight and I saw George's panicked expression. I reached out and gave her hand a reassuring squeeze. "It's okay," I mouthed at her. I'd been in situations like this before, and I really wasn't too worried. People didn't often look under their beds.

"Okay. Call me if you need me," Kyle said, and ended the call. His feet disappeared as he swung them up onto the bed, sighing yet again. I guessed he was going for five minutes' rest. Inconvenient and uncomfortable, but still nothing to worry about—as long as neither George nor I had a sudden uncontrollable need to sneeze.

There was a thud and I saw Kyle's PDA land on the carpet. He must have dropped it by accident. Grumbling under his breath, he sat up again. His feet came down—and his heel hit the PDA and knocked it under the bed!

Suddenly I couldn't breathe. The PDA lay there, about two inches from my face. If he looked under the bed . . .

I held my breath and tried not to move even a hair as Kyle's hand reached under the dust ruffle. I watched in horrified fascination as it groped around right in front of my nose! Don't touch me, don't touch me, don't touch me, I chanted to myself.

Then Kyle's fingers closed on the PDA and he withdrew his arm. Slowly, silently, I let out my breath. When I looked over at George, she was staring at me, frozen. Then, still silently, her shoulders began to shake and her face contorted. She put a hand over her mouth. Her face turned red.

I couldn't believe it. She was cracking up!

I glared at her, willing her not to make a sound, as above us Kyle stood up, moved to the desk chair, and took his suit jacket off the back. At last, thankfully, he left the room. The door clicked shut.

Just in time. A loud snorting sound burst out from behind George's hand. "Oh, wow!" she gasped. "Sorry, Nan, but suddenly the whole situation just seemed completely hilarious!"

I gave her a frosty look and wiggled out from under the bed. "I'm glad you had your fun," I said severely. "Remind me not to take you on any more illegal activities. You obviously have a strange way of handling stress."

"Sorry." Still giggling, George crawled out from under the bed, stood up, and brushed herself off. "Okay. Let's do what we came here to do, what do you say?"

I waved at Kyle's computer, which was indeed sitting on the desk. "Be my guest."

While she was getting started, I quickly opened the room door and hung the "do not disturb" sign on the knob, just in case the maid was making the evening turndown rounds now.

As George worked, I prowled around the room, but there wasn't much to look at. Kyle obviously hadn't spent much time here.

"Oh, puh-leeze," George groaned. "Too easy! Guess what Kyle's password is?"

"Uh—Prettyface?" I suggested.

"Nope. PrincessK. As in, Kelly," George said, rolling her eyes. "The guy needs to get a life— and stop living his daughter's life for her."

I peered over George's shoulder at the screen. "So have you found the e-mail we're looking for?"

"Not yet." George scrolled rapidly through Kyle's Sent folder. "It's not in here, which isn't surprising. If he did send it, he'd have had to log in as Anna, so there wouldn't be a copy of it in any of his e-mail folders. But that doesn't mean there's no record of it anywhere on his computer. You just have to know where to look."

She typed a few keys, scanned a few more screens. Then she sat back in the chair and gave me a satisfied smile. "Ta-dah," she said. "In the browser cache."

I looked at the screen again. And there it was—"Anna's" e-mail. "So Kyle did send it!" I murmured, my skin prickling. Here it was—our first actual evidence that Anna's disappearance was not what it seemed to be. And that, whatever had really happened to her, Kyle McMahon was involved.

I checked the time stamp. The message had been sent at 7:30 a.m.—half an hour before Anna and I were supposed to meet! So whatever happened to her, it must have already happened by then.

"George, is there a way you can save this info and send it to your computer?" I asked. "It's the only proof we have so far."

"I think so. I just have to translate it into plain text." George hit some more keys, then highlighted the whole message, including the time stamp and the various identifiers proving that it came from Kyle's computer, and copied it into an e-mail. She hit Send, then opened the Sent folder and deleted it. "Unless he's a computer geek, he'll never know we were here," she promised me.

Before she shut the computer down, I asked George to show me one more thing—Kyle's schedule. She brought up the calendar screen and I peered at it. Wow. Kyle had had meetings last night until a dinner that started at 7:30. And then he'd had meetings again this morning, starting with a working breakfast with his staff at 7:00!

"So did he send the e-mail during his staff meeting?" George wondered. "That's unbelievably cold-blooded!"

I had to agree, it was hard to believe. I was starting to wonder just exactly when Kyle had found the time to fit in a kidnapping. He was one busy man!

Just then my cell phone vibrated from my jeans pocket. I fished it out and saw that I had two text messages. One was from Ned, with a fax number. The second was from Bess.

"'Following Kelly 2 secret meeting!'" I read aloud. "'Come quick!'"

"Time to motor," George said.

As she shut Kyle's computer down, I made a last-minute sweep of the room to be sure we'd left no sign of ourselves there. Then we hurried out. "Where r u?" I texted Bess.

"8th St. & 5th Ave." came the answer.

"On our way," I wrote back.

With Bess texting us her new position every couple of minutes and George finding the locations on her PDA, we wove through the streets of New York. We were moving slowly east.

We finally caught up with Bess on St. Mark's Place in the East Village. She was loitering by a window display of shoes across the street from a restaurant called JoEllen's Kitchen. "Don't look," she told us immediately. "She's in there at the table by the window." She jerked her head backward to indicate the restaurant.

"By herself?" I asked, disappointed.

"I think she's waiting for someone," Bess explained. "She's been in there for about fifteen minutes and I don't think she's ordered anything. The waitress keeps coming by and refilling her water."

"Nice work," I said. "What else did you find out today?"

"Kelly does seem to be acting pretty squirrelly," Bess said. "I stopped by your room pretending I was looking for you and she was superfriendly, like she usually is. We hung out and chatted for a while, and I got some info about what her dad was doing last night—I'll tell you about that in a second—then I asked her what she was doing tonight and she totally clammed up. I didn't want to get her wondering about what I was up to, so I just said good-bye and left. I waited in the lobby until she came out and followed her."

"Smart!" I told her.

"So what should we do now?" Bess asked.

"We wait and see who she's meeting with," I explained. "We might want to move to a different window—there's only so long we can look at shoes without seeming suspicious."

"Oh, I don't know. I could look at them all day," Bess remarked. "Although these"—she shot a glance at the display, which was full of studded combat boots and vampy platform shoes in various extreme colors"—are not exactly my style, I have to say."

"I think the glittery red ones with the six-inch heel are totally you," George said.

I laughed. "Come on, let's keep moving up and down the street. As long as we can still see her window, we'll be okay."

"Oh, I forgot to tell you in all the excitement—your friend Officer Johansen gave me two names of protesters who got arrested," George told me as we strolled down the street. "I got in touch with one of them—a guy named Mark Breedlove who's a student at one of the local colleges."

"You guys are so efficient!" I said appreciatively. I glanced back at the restaurant window. Kelly was still alone. "So what did he have to say?"

"Something pretty interesting," George replied.

"Which is . . . ?" I prompted when she paused.

She looked satisfied. "Well. He was kind of bitter because he's not really into animal rights himself. He just went along with it because this girl he likes is into it. Then he got arrested, and she *didn't* get arrested, and she didn't even come to bail him out!"

"Bummer," Bess commented.

"Yeah. So anyway, he was happy to spill whatever he knew. And guess what he said?" George paused expectantly.

"I have no idea!" I protested, punching her lightly on the arm. "Would you quit with the suspense?"

"He said . . ." George paused once more, then went on, "He said that the person who came to the animal-rights group with all the info about Pretty Face was someone connected with the pageant!"

Bess and I both gasped.

George grinned. "I know. It's an inside job. Scandalous, right?"

"Someone connected with the pageant? Who?" I demanded.

"He didn't know her name. He only saw her once, the night of the 'happening' at the Horatio," George said. "But he says she was about our age, and petite, and blond."

My heart sank. Kelly was petite and blond. Of

course, there were other people connected with the pageant who were petite and blond too, but no one else that I knew of who'd been acting as suspicious as Kelly had.

Only I still couldn't figure out *why* she would be trying to sabotage her own father's company on the sly. . . .

I glanced back at the restaurant window again—and did a double take. While George had been talking, Kelly's dinner companion had arrived. Kelly was leaning across the table, her face intent as she said something to him.

We moved closer and I could see that Kelly's friend was a guy of about eighteen, with a scraggly black goatee and longish hair that he kept pushing out of his eyes. He wore an ancient blue T-shirt that read SAVE THE WHALES. He was gazing at Kelly with a soulful expression.

"Oh, that guy is definitely an animal-rights protester," Bess murmured. "Look how thin he is. He's probably a vegetarian."

I sighed. I wasn't looking forward to this—I really liked Kelly, and I didn't want to get her in trouble—but I had to confront her and find out once and for all what she was up to. Especially if she could shed some light on Anna Chavez's disappearance.

"Come on," I said. Squaring my shoulders, I walked into the restaurant and marched up to Kelly's table. Bess and George were right behind me.

"Hello, Kelly," I said.

She glanced up and her face turned white. "What—how—," she began.

I folded my arms. "Kelly, is there something you want to tell me?"

THE WRONG ANSWERS

"Oh, no!" Kelly said. Reaching up, she grasped my arm. Her blue eyes were huge. "Nancy, please, don't tell my dad about this!"

My heart sank another few inches. More proof that I'd been right.

"I don't want to tell on you," I said quietly. "But I don't understand why you're doing this. Maybe if you tried to explain it to me . . ."

"Kelly, who are these people?" the guy asked, looking bewildered. "What's going on?"

"Oh, like you don't know, Mr. Animal Activist," Bess said darkly.

"Huh?" the guy said, staring back at Bess.

A waitress walked up with a loaded tray. "Your

bacon cheeseburger," she said, setting a plate down in front of the skinny guy. "And your Cobb salad," she said, putting a bowl in front of Kelly.

"A bacon cheeseburger!" Bess cried, outraged. "You hypocrite! Do your friends at PETA know about this?"

"*What?*" the guy said, looking alarmed now. "Pita? You mean the flatbread? What are you talking about?"

"Why would you want to ruin Pretty Face, Kelly?" George asked. "I just don't get it."

"*What?*" Kelly demanded. And then everyone was talking at once.

"Hold on, hold on," I called, raising my hands for silence. I was starting to think something was seriously off. "I think we're misunderstanding each other."

As soon as everyone was quiet, I turned back to Kelly. "What is it you don't want me to mention to your dad?" I asked.

Kelly reached across the table and took the skinny guy's hand. "This is Andrew." She introduced us. "He's from River Heights. We used to date."

"Okay," I said slowly. "And . . . ?"

"And, well, my dad didn't exactly approve. For

one thing, Andrew's older—he's in college now," Kelly went on.

I could think of a bunch of other reasons Kyle wouldn't approve of Andrew. But the main one was that, in Kyle's eyes, no boy would ever be good enough to date Kelly.

"Anyway, Daddy made me stop seeing him." Kelly gave Andrew a shy smile. "But I didn't stop caring about him. So when I got to New York, I called him and we made plans to see each other tonight. It was bad to go behind Daddy's back, I know. But I just had to."

"Oh," Bess said in a small voice. "So, uh, Andrew, you're not an animal-rights activist, I guess."

"Um, no," he replied, still staring at her as if she were insane. "I'm a computer science major."

"Wait. You thought *I* was involved with those nutty protesters?" Kelly asked. She gave an incredulous laugh. "Why in the world would you think that?"

"Excuse me, but are you girls going to sit down?" the waitress asked. "Because you're blocking the way here."

"Kelly, do you mind if we share your booth for a minute?" I asked. "I just need to clear a few things up."

Kelly hesitated, but then she and Andrew slid over on the booth seats to make room for us.

"The night of the first protest, I found an empty tube of stage blood in our bathroom garbage," I explained to Kelly.

"How could you think I'd sabotage my own father?" Kelly asked me. She sounded angry. "I don't know where the stage blood came from. But I can't believe you, Nancy! I thought we were friends. But you seem to think I'm capable of being some kind of sneaky criminal."

"I'm sorry. I really am," I said. Suddenly I felt incredibly tired and confused. "It's just that there was the tube of blood, and then when I asked you about the protest, you got all nervous and said you hadn't seen it—"

"That was because I sneaked out of the reception to call Andrew," Kelly told me. "I really didn't see it. Is that the only reason you suspected me?" She sounded hurt.

"No," I said gently. "You acted so secretive every time I asked you if you wanted to do something with me. I guess I thought you were hiding something from me." I shrugged. "Which turns out to be the case."

Kelly looked ashamed. "I guess that's true," she murmured. "I was afraid I'd jinx things if I told anyone what I was doing. I was sort of afraid that Andrew wouldn't want to see me again."

"Are you nuts?" Andrew said, taking her hand. "Of course I wanted to see you!"

Kelly gave him a smile. "I know that now, but I didn't then." She turned back to me. "Plus I felt bad about deceiving my dad. That's why I didn't tell you what I was up to. I guess I was acting a little weird. I'm sorry, Nancy."

"Me too," I told her.

"But there's more," George said. "Today we talked to someone who told us that the person who masterminded the protests was a Pretty Face pageant insider. Someone our age, with blond hair."

"There's at least four girls in the pageant with blond hair," Kelly pointed out. "Me, Piper, Cheryl Amery, Madison Lane—"

"Piper," I said as something finally clicked in my mind. "Why didn't I think of that sooner? Of course, Piper!"

"You think Piper is the one?" George asked.

"Well, she's blond, she's petite, she's a pageant insider. *And* I just remembered the key point. She was in our room the night of the first protest, wasn't she?" I said. I glanced at Kelly. "Didn't you say she was one of the girls who came up to hang out after the party? She could have left the empty tube in our garbage can then."

"Yeah," Kelly said, frowning. "But why? Why would *she* want to hurt Pretty Face?"

"I don't know if you noticed, but Piper has been pretty bitter ever since I won the crown," I said. "She seems to think it was rightfully hers. Put that together with what happened to her sister—"

"You mean Robin?" Kelly asked. Robin Depken had been the runner-up Miss Pretty Face River Heights the previous year, when Kelly had won. Kelly had actually won Miss Congeniality to start with, but then both the winner of the crown, Portia Leoni, and the runner-up, Robin Depken, had been disqualified. Portia had been framed for shoplifting, and Robin had been disqualified because one of the judges admitted to skewing the votes in Robin's favor, though that hadn't been Robin's fault. In the end, Kelly had ended up taking the crown.

"Yes. Between Robin being disqualified and Piper losing to me, I could see why Piper might start to think the contest was rigged against her family," I said.

"So she wanted to take revenge," George suggested.

"Maybe," I agreed.

"I'm not sure I believe that," Kelly objected. "Piper hasn't seemed negative at all about being the runner-up. Nancy, I have to tell you, I think you're overly suspicious."

I sighed. "I guess I need to talk to Piper. But carefully." After my false conclusion with Kelly, I wasn't about to accuse anyone else without unshakable proof. I just hoped Kelly could forgive me.

Although, since it now seemed almost certain her father was involved with Anna Chavez's disappearance, chances were Kelly was going to have much bigger reasons to be upset with me soon. . . .

The thought made me feel even more exhausted. Suddenly all I wanted was to go back to the hotel, crawl into bed, and stay there for a week.

That was the moment at which Kelly, checking her watch, turned to me with a frown. "Nancy, it's eight fifteen," she said. "Doesn't the party at Club Mirador start pretty soon?"

I looked at my own watch and gasped. Oh, no! In the excitement of the evening, I had forgotten about tonight's event: the pre-pageant press party at the club. The party started at nine o'clock, but all the contestants were supposed to be there at eight thirty. That was in fifteen minutes—and the club was all the way over on West 57th Street. If I'd learned one thing about New York City, it was that there was no way to get from the East Village, where we were, to West 57th Street in fifteen minutes. Not to mention the fact that I was still in my jeans, a white tank top under my denim jacket, and sneakers, and not wearing any makeup.

I slid down in my seat and groaned. "That's it. I'm done. Looks like Piper can have the crown after all. Harrison Hendrickson will make sure I'm kicked out of the pageant after this."

There was silence around the table. Then Bess smacked her palm down on the tabletop.

"No!" she declared. "I'm not going to let that happen!"

George turned to stare at her. "Excuse me, but what exactly are *you* planning to do to stop it?"

"There's no time to explain," Bess said. She leaned forward and put her hand on my arm. "Nancy, we can still save the situation," she said urgently. "All you have to do is trust me—and do exactly as I say."

MAKEOVER ON THE MOVE

"**U**h—okay," I said to Bess. I didn't have the faintest idea what she was up to, but I knew she was serious. "I trust you. Tell me what to do."

"Kelly, switch shoes with Nancy, please," Bess directed rapidly. "We already know your feet are the same size from when you loaned Nancy your tennis sneakers. And we'll need your jacket, too, I'm sorry."

"Why are you switching clothes?" Andrew asked plaintively.

"Because Kelly is nicely dressed for her date with you," Bess told him, "and we need to glam Nancy up fast."

I was already putting on Kelly's shoes, which

were heeled sandals that actually looked really good with my jeans. I pulled on her jacket, a below-the-hip blazer in dark blue velvet, and handed her my denim jacket.

"Let's go," Bess commanded, grabbing my hand.

"Thanks, Kelly," I gasped over my shoulder as Bess hauled me outside. George was following, looking as startled as I felt.

"Good luck!" Kelly said.

"Uh—nice to meet you," Adam called after us.

Bess stood on the curb and stuck her hand in the air. A taxi drew to a halt down the street from us and a couple started toward it. Bess ran forward and grabbed the door.

"This is an emergency," she told the couple sternly. "I'm sorry, but you'll have to catch the next taxi." She opened the door, then waved George and me inside. "Let's go, not a moment to waste!"

"Where to?" asked the driver, a young man in a turban.

"Club Mirador on West Fifty-seventh Street," Bess said. "And if you can get us there before eight thirty, I'll pay you ten dollars extra."

"Not a problem," said the driver, and pulled away from the curb with a screech of tires.

"Bess," I said nervously as we zoomed down St. Mark's Place, "this seems kind of dangerous. Oof!" We hit a pothole and bounced.

"He knows what he's doing," Bess assured me. "Plus, taxis all have V-8 engines and extrastrong shocks. They use the same model they use for police cars. We'll be fine."

One of the weird but wonderful things about Bess is that she knows a ton about cars.

"I don't think Nancy was worried about us so much as the pedestrians—and other vehicle operators," George murmured as we narrowly missed ramming a bicycle messenger who jumped the traffic light.

"If they're going to break the traffic laws, then they'll have to take the consequences," Bess snapped. She was rummaging in her bag. A second later she pulled out her makeup case and ripped the top off a sampler of Perfect Face. "Turn toward me, Nan."

Obedient—or, rather, stunned—I turned my face and let Bess smooth the shimmery lotion onto my cheeks. The familiar tingle spread over my skin.

"Good," Bess murmured. "Now your eyes." Pulling out a blue liner pencil, she quickly and expertly lined my eyes. I cringed, expecting every second to have my eye poked out. But miraculously it didn't happen.

"Good thing you and I wear the same makeup colors," Bess said, steadying her hand against my cheek as the taxi jolted along. She stroked on a coat of mascara.

"Yeah, I guess so," I managed to say while she patted blush onto the apples of my cheeks.

"No talking," she chided, and started outlining my lips with a different liner pencil. She filled in the outline, then applied shimmery gloss over everything. "Whoops!" she said as we bounced over a bump. Pulling a cotton swab from her makeup bag, she dabbed at the gloss that had smeared onto my cheek. "No problem."

"It's eight twenty-two, and we're only at Thirty-first Street," George informed us.

"I can go faster," the driver called eagerly. The engine roared and the car surged forward even more swiftly.

"Is the mascara dry yet? Can I shut my eyes?" I asked. "Because I'm afraid to look!"

"You have to shut your eyes anyway, because I need to put some shadow on them," Bess told me. "But I'm telling you, Nancy, we're perfectly fine. The driver is a pro. And so am I.

"Okay, open now," she said a minute later. I

opened my eyes to find her and George staring at me with considering looks on their faces.

"That's pretty amazing, I have to admit," George said after a moment.

"Thanks, but I'm not done yet," Bess said. She pulled out a hairbrush. "Flip your head upside down, Nan."

I did as I was told. I felt the brush tugging at the roots of my hair. Then Bess ordered me to flip upright again.

"See? It's all nice and full now," she said approvingly.

Reaching into her bag once more, she pulled out a gorgeous necklace of twisted silver wire and gemlike bits of glass. "I bought this on Saint Mark's Place while I was waiting for you guys," she told us. She unclasped it and fastened it around my neck. "It looks perfect with your outfit, Nancy!"

Digging into her bag once more, she came out with a compact mirror and handed it to me. "Check yourself out."

I peered at my reflection. I had to admit, I looked really good. My makeup looked professional, the necklace looked fantastic with the velvet blazer, and even my tank top and jeans seemed like they were part of the plan.

"You are some kind of wizard," I told Bess.

"The scary kind," George chimed in. "In a good way, of course."

"I can't believe you pulled this all together so fast, and out of nowhere!" I added.

"It's a talent," Bess said modestly.

"Eight twenty-eight," George called.

"We are almost there, don't worry, ladies! I will not fail you!" the driver cried. He seemed to have entered fully into the spirit of the adventure.

We tore around a corner and then shuddered to a halt in front of Club Mirador. Bess threw the cab door open and let me out. "You run in," she ordered me. "George and I will pay the driver. We'll see you later at the hotel."

I gave her a quick hug. "My heroes. Thanks a million!"

As I slipped inside the club, my watch told me it was 8:30 exactly. I spotted the other contestants and made myself walk demurely toward them. I stopped next to Piper and Raven. Piper scowled at me. Harrison Hendrickson caught my eye and gave me a tiny nod.

Phew!

The event was, frankly, sort of a blur. I was exhausted—it seemed like this day had gone on for at least a week—and I was also distracted with thinking about my case, or cases. I couldn't stop staring at Kyle McMahon. He was schmoozing and smiling like he always did, but I could see the lines of exhaustion and stress on his face. Was it really possible that he'd had Anna Chavez kidnapped? He really didn't seem like the criminal type. Then again, the evidence we'd found on his computer was pretty much unarguable.

I also wanted to question Piper about the protests and see if I could get her to reveal anything, but every time I came near her she would walk away from me. This was going to be tricky, since she so clearly didn't like me. She was going to like me even less when I accused her of trying to sabotage Pretty Face. But I had to get her to tell me what she knew. It might lead to my finding Anna.

I listened while Kyle made a speech about Pretty Face. He talked a lot about how Pretty Face had grown in the last few years. "As most of you know, we're building new corporate headquarters on Albany Street in downtown Manhattan, and we've almost finished construction on the office tower," he said. "I went to visit the building site earlier today and it is spectacular—a state-of-the-art facility with its own product-testing labs, all constructed with green technology." A sudden grin broke across his face. "It is really amazing. It's even got a helicopter landing pad on the roof!"

The crowd laughed appreciatively. Then Kyle's grin faded and he looked earnest again. "Seriously—what a boon for the city! Our company is one of the leaders in helping to revive the economy of that area."

He went on to talk about what a good corporate citizen Pretty Face was, with its eco-friendly products and its many charitable and community outreach programs—the pageant being one of them. "The pageant is a win for everyone," he said. "Pretty Face gets lovely, fresh-faced young ambassadors for its product line, the contestants who win the regional titles get scholarships and a lifetime supply of our wonderful cosmetics, the one who wins the national title gets a trip around the world and much more, and everyone's happy."

I glanced at Piper, who was standing near me in the crowd. Her face wore a sneer. Then, as she noticed me looking at her, she smoothed it out into a bland smile.

There's one person who's not happy, I thought.

A second later I caught myself stifling a huge yawn. Man, I was tired!

As soon as I could decently do it, I slipped away from the party and caught a taxi back to the hotel. I went straight to Bess and George's room, where they were waiting for me.

"So, how'd it go?" Bess asked.

"Well, no one yelled at me," I said, "which is about the best I was hoping for. So I guess it went well. Thanks again, Bess. You saved my life!"

I yawned again. The day was catching up with me in a big way. And tomorrow evening was the pageant. I needed to get my beauty sleep—but more important, I needed to figure out what had happened to Anna Chavez!

"So before I forget, tell me what Kelly said about her dad's activities last night," I urged as I helped myself to a diet soda from the minibar.

"Well, it was pretty easy to get her on to the subject," Bess said. "All I had to do was say that her dad seemed to be working really hard. Kelly went off about how stressed he was, how the new job was really wearing him out, how he seemed so worried all the time, how she had barely even seen him since we got to New York."

I nodded. "That's saying something," I commented. "When we were back in River Heights, he hovered over her all the time."

"She told me he'd been working the phones or in meetings solidly all evening," Bess went on. "He had to deal with the animal-rights protest thing, then he had a dinner with the Pretty Face sales team that lasted till like nine thirty, then he came back to the hotel and did more work. She stopped in to see him at ten and again at eleven and both times he was on the phone and couldn't talk."

"That must have been after I fell asleep," I said. I hadn't even heard her leave.

"So if he kidnapped Anna, he must have done it after eleven last night, is that what we're saying?" George asked.

"Actually, he must have done it after twelve thirty," Bess told us. She looked triumphant. "I checked with the night desk clerk. I wanted to know if he saw Kyle leave the hotel after eleven. He said he never saw him leave, and then he called the room service people and they said Kyle ordered a club sandwich at midnight. It was delivered at twelve twenty-five and he signed for it in person."

"Wow!" I exclaimed, amazed. "Bess, how did you get the clerk to tell you all this stuff? They're totally not supposed to share that kind of information."

Bess grinned and batted her eyelashes. "I have my methods."

"Unbelievable," George said with a snort.

I thought back to the schedule I'd seen on Kyle's computer, which said he'd had a breakfast meeting this morning. "Okay. So from what we know, it seems that Kyle could only have kidnapped Anna sometime between about one a.m. and six thirty a.m. today," I said. I frowned. "Which is weird, because there was no sign of forced entry or a struggle in Anna's apartment. He would have had to buzz her and get her to let him into her apartment in the middle of the night, and then get her to leave with him."

"And then he would have had to take her wherever he was taking her," George added.

"And be at the office in time for his seven a.m. staff meeting," I finished. "How did he do it all?"

"Maybe he canceled the staff meeting," Bess suggested.

I thought back to what I'd overheard Kyle say to his product manager about the meeting while George and I were hiding under his bed. "No, it happened."

"Maybe he had help," George said.

I nodded. It was what I'd been thinking too. What if someone were in this with Kyle? Someone like Adam Bedrossian?

If that was the case, I had a feeling we were moving into much more dangerous territory. . . .

And the crazy thing was, I still didn't even know *why*. Why had Anna gone missing? What was it that she and Kyle had argued about that night at the reception? What had she wanted to talk to me about?

What was so important that Kyle needed to get her out of the way?

"I wish I could go back to that reception and just go through the whole thing again," I muttered. "I feel like I wasn't paying enough attention, or not paying attention to the right things, or something."

George snapped her fingers. "You can't go back in time, Nan, but we do have something that might be almost as good." Opening the drawer of her bedside table, she pulled out her camcorder. "I recorded it, remember?"

"George, I love you!" I yelped, and snatched the camcorder out of her hands. "How do you play back the video on this thing?"

"Easy, cowboy. Leave the techno stuff to me,

okay?" George took the machine back and carried it over to her laptop. She took out a cable and hooked the camcorder up to the computer.

Bess and I gathered around as the film began to play. The camera's view was a little jerky, and George had added occasional low-voiced, snarky comments on what people were wearing and talking about.

"George, is there a way to get rid of your voice-over?" I asked. "I'd like to see if we might be able to overhear some of the party."

"Sorry," George said. "I might be able to do it in a video editing lab, but not here."

We reached the moment where the lights went out and the protest started. "Wait. Back up five minutes or so," I instructed. "I want to find Piper and see if we can track her movements."

George obediently rewound to five minutes earlier. She advanced the film slowly while I scanned the room for Piper's red dress. In a moment I spotted her, standing by herself. She was too far away for me to see her expression. But I caught my breath as I saw her glance at her watch, then make for one of the exits. At the doorway she paused, looking around as if to make sure no one was watching her. Then she slipped out.

"She left, and three minutes later the protest started," I murmured. "She's the one who set it up. She has to be!"

We kept watching. The party continued, then the lights went out. This time I focused on the protesters, trying my best to make out their faces under the fake blood. Was one of them Piper?

No. There were three girls on the stage, but all of them were too tall and the wrong body type. Besides, there was no way she'd have had time to change out of her party outfit in the time between when she'd gone out and when the protest started.

"Did you know they test their products on helpless animals?" the distorted voice cried.

"That voice . . . ," I said, frowning.

"Oh, come on," Bess objected. "It's so distorted. You can't tell me you recognize it."

"Not the voice itself, but the accent," I said. "The way it says 'product' and 'animals' with kind of long vowels. That's a Midwestern accent."

George made a face. "Do you think that's enough to go on?"

"No," I said with a sigh. I was *so* tired. "I need real proof—a smoking gun."

"So how do you think they did that voice distortion, George?" Bess asked.

"It's easy," George said. "Anyone can download voice-changing software off the Internet. You can make yourself sound like a warrior princess, or a demon, or pretty much anything you can think of. There are hundreds of programs. People use it for online gaming, mostly. But I'm sure that's what they used here. In fact, it sounds like one of the 'evil creature' voices from a program called VoxPop. I have that program."

"Is there any way to reverse the distortion?" I asked.

George's brow furrowed as she thought about it. "You know, maybe I can," she said slowly. "Hang on, let me try something. . . ."

Turning to her keyboard, she began typing furiously. A few moments later she said, "Let's try this."

She hit a button and a voice filled the air again. "Did you know they test their products on helpless animals?"

Bess and I burst out laughing. This time the voice sounded like a demented pixie.

"Okay, so that wasn't quite right," George said with a grin. "Let me try something else. . . ."

She made a few changes, then held up a hand. "How about this?"

Once again we heard, "Did you know they test their products on helpless animals?"

I gasped. This time the voice was human.

And it was definitely the voice of one Piper Depken.

10

THE FROG CONNECTION

"**G**eorge, you did it!" I cried, leaping up to hug my friend. "There's the proof I need!"

"I don't know if it would hold up in court," George cautioned. "I just played a second voice program on top of the first. They canceled each other out, sort of."

"I don't need it to hold up in court," I said. "All I need is to convince Piper that she's been exposed, so she'll tell me what she knows."

I checked the clock. It was 11:30. Technically, that was pretty late to go knocking on someone's door, but I had a mystery to solve, and a missing girl to find.

Piper's room was on the floor above. Borrowing George's laptop, I hurried up the stairs and knocked on Piper's door. Her voice called, "Who is it?"

"Nancy Drew," I called back. "Piper, I need to talk to you. It's important."

A moment passed and then the door swung open. Piper stood there scowling at me. She was still in her party clothes.

"What?" she demanded.

I pushed past her and set the laptop down on her desk. "Listen to this," I said, and pressed Play on George's sound file.

"Did you know they test their products on helpless animals?" rang out one more time. Piper's eyes widened.

"I know it was you," I told her quietly. "That's your voice."

Piper's face turned pale. Then the color began to come back into it in blotchy patches.

"So what if it was me?" she snarled. "It's not against the law."

"No, but I'm sure Pretty Face wouldn't look too kindly on you trying to smear their reputation," I said. "They'd boot you from the pageant for sure."

"Fine, then, let them," Piper shot back. "It wouldn't matter. I already know this whole pageant is rotten. They have it in for me and my family. And so do you, apparently."

"I know you won't believe me, but I really don't, Piper," I told her. "And I'm not doing this for Pretty Face. I mean, I don't understand why you did it and I'm certainly not condoning your actions, but that's not my main concern right now. I just need to know what you know about this animal-testing stuff, and where you got your info."

"That crown was mine. You stole it from me," Piper snapped. She folded her arms and stared defiantly at me. "Why should I tell you anything?"

"Because a woman's life could be in danger," I said urgently.

Piper's mouth fell open. "What are you talking about?"

I grasped her arm. "Listen to me. Anna Chavez has disappeared. And I think it has something to do with the protest you staged. You have to tell me—did you get your information from her?"

"Anna who?" Piper looked bewildered now. "I don't even know who that is."

My heart sank. I'd been hoping the connection would be clear—Anna told Piper about animal testing, Kyle found out, Kyle took steps to silence Anna. But apparently it wasn't that simple. Taking a deep breath, I moved to one of the chairs and sat down. "Okay, never mind about that. Just, please, tell me what you do know. It could be important."

"My sister, Robin, told me about the animal testing," Piper explained, eyeing me uncertainly. "She found out something about Perfect Face last year. I think she read an e-mail she wasn't supposed to, one day when she was at Kelly's house."

My attention sharpened. "Go on."

"Robin said they were using frogs somehow to make the new Perfect Face," Piper went on. "The e-mail said something about how not enough testing had been done and they ought to delay putting the product on the market." She shrugged. "Robin thought the e-mail meant they were, like, testing the stuff on frogs. She was grossed out. She tried to get me to stop using Pretty Face products. But I figured, well, if it works, who cares if it's tested on frogs?"

I blinked and tried to keep my face neutral.

"But then after I lost the crown, I got mad," Piper went on. "I mean, it's obvious that Pretty Face just didn't want me or my sister to be their spokesperson, and that's totally unfair. So I decided to get revenge."

"Okay," I prompted.

"See, Pretty Face goes on and on about how they're eco-friendly, but they're big hypocrites, because they're testing their stuff on frogs and that's hardly eco-friendly, is it? I mean, frogs are, like, endangered and all."

I'd never heard that frogs were endangered, actually. Not as an entire genus, anyway. But I didn't want to interrupt the flow, so I kept quiet.

"I wanted to show that they were hypocrites, but I didn't think people would care so much about frogs. I mean, lots of people don't like frogs. They're gross." Piper held up one finger. "But *everyone* loves cute little bunnies."

"So you staged the protest, but you changed the frogs to bunnies," I guessed.

Piper nodded. "I found some animal-rights groups on the Web and picked the one that did the most outrageous protests," she said. "That's pretty much it."

I sat there in silence, thinking about what I'd just learned.

The bad news was, Piper didn't know Anna, and really didn't know anything about Pretty Face and animal testing. Her only proof was an unspecific e-mail that she hadn't even read herself.

On the other hand, the e-mail had mentioned

frogs. I thought of the article in Spanish I'd found in Anna's desk drawer. That was about frogs, too. Coincidence? Surely not.

So maybe there *was* some dirty secret about animal testing at Pretty Face—just not the one Piper had tried to publicize. Was that what Anna had wanted to talk to me about?

Then again, Anna's lab mate, Marty Anders, had been so definite about Pretty Face not doing animal testing. He should know—and I couldn't see why he'd lie about it.

I felt like clutching my head in frustration. This case was so confusing!

"So . . ." Piper broke the silence. Studying her fingernails, her voice deceptively casual, she asked, "Uh . . . you don't really need to turn me in to Kyle, do you? I mean, if I promise to call off the protest group?"

I stared at her in surprise. "Would it matter? I thought you wanted to expose Pretty Face. What do you care if you get kicked out of the pageant?"

"Well . . ." Piper still didn't look at me. "I am still runner-up. And let's be honest, you haven't exactly been impressing Harrison Hendrickson. I might be . . . needed."

I stood up to leave. "I won't tell anyone if I

don't have to," I said, too weary to argue.

Collecting George's laptop, I got out of there as fast as I could. When this case was over, I was going to get as far from the pageant world as I could.

I went to my room. There was one last thing I had to do tonight before I could finally fall into bed. Rummaging through my purse, I found the article I'd taken from Anna's desk. I took the elevator down to the hotel lobby, where the business center was.

The center was deserted at this hour, but luckily it wasn't locked up and the machines were all still on. At the fax machine I grabbed a cover sheet and scribbled a quick note to Ned. "Urgent!! Too tired to explain right now, but can you please find someone in the Spanish Department at the U. to translate this article ASAP, and then fax translation back to me? It's for a case. Of course. Love you, miss you. N"

Putting the note and the magazine page into the fax feeder, I dialed the fax number Ned had given me and hit Send.

The machine whirred and beeped, the pages fed slowly through. A second later a message flashed on the tiny LCD screen: DATA SENT.

I waited for a confirmation to print out, but nothing happened. Then I saw that the screen was flashing another message: ADD PAPER.

The fax printer must be out of paper. Well, I was too tired to hunt around for some hotel staff person to reload it right now. I didn't need the confirmation, anyway—the machine had confirmed the fax was sent.

I headed out toward the elevator again. As I pressed the Up button, I suddenly got the strangest feeling I was being watched. Turning, I glanced around the lobby.

A chill washed over me. There, standing by a column with his arms folded, was Adam Bedrossian. He was gazing steadily at me, his face as unreadable as ever.

How long had he been there? Was he following me? Or was I just being paranoid?

The elevator arrived and I stepped on. As the doors slid closed, I peeked out one last time and saw that he was still there, watching.

The next morning I slept until eight thirty. I'd fallen asleep before Kelly got in the night before, and she was already gone by the time I woke up. I felt bad—I wondered if she was avoiding me after the accusation I'd made yesterday about her involvement in the protests. I told myself that now wasn't the time to think about that.

Since today was pageant day, we had very little on our schedules. All I had was an afternoon spa session at one o'clock. Then I was free until the pageant itself, that night at eight o'clock—which meant that I could spend the bulk of the day trying to find out what had become of Anna.

I knew Bess and George weren't around this morning—they were visiting their great-aunt Estelle, who lived on the Upper West Side. Great-Aunt Estelle is a little crazy, but I like her a lot. Ordinarily I would have gone with them to see her, but between the pageant and my case I couldn't spare the time.

I dressed quickly, then hurried down to the business center. No fax from Ned yet. Well, I supposed it was still pretty early. I went up to the hotel's rooftop café and ordered a light breakfast—fruit and yogurt, a muffin, and a latte. I sat there sipping the latte and enjoying one of the first quiet moments I'd had since I came to New York. If only I wasn't so worried about Anna!

As I was leaving the restaurant, my cell phone rang. I checked the caller ID. Ned!

I flicked open the phone. "I was hoping it would be you," I said. "Did you get my fax?"

"Yes, I got it," Ned said. "Oh, and by the way, good morning. I miss you."

I smiled into the phone. Ned's voice always comforted me. "I miss you too."

"That's better. Okay, back to business—I got your fax and sent you a reply hours ago. Yours came through at midnight, my time, and since I happened to be studying with my friend Vicente, I gave it to him and he translated it on the spot. Then he faxed the translation back to you from his computer. It must have been about one in the morning."

I frowned. "That's weird. I checked at the business center and they didn't have anything for me. Are you sure it went through?"

"Yeah, Vicente got a confirmation," Ned said. "I can call him and ask him to send it again, but he's in class right now, so it won't be for a couple of hours."

I bit my lip. "Can you give me a recap? I don't have a lot of time to spare." Glancing around, I spotted a small seating area near the elevator. I went and sat down in one of the armchairs. "Okay, I'm ready for you."

"Nan, you've had some weird cases, but if this article is anything to go by, this has got to be one of your weirder ones," Ned said. "The article is about cosmetic uses of the venom secreted by certain frogs."

"Cosmetic uses of frog venom!" My pulse sped up. "Go on."

"I see this means something to you. Should I worry?" Ned joked. "Well, apparently there's a species of Venezuelan tree frog that defends itself by covering its skin with a neurotoxin that paralyzes anything that tries to eat it. The chemical properties of this neurotoxin happen to be very similar to those of Botox."

"Botox?" I exclaimed. "You mean the stuff that people inject into their faces to keep from getting wrinkles?"

"That's the stuff," Ned confirmed. "Actually, it's not as surprising as it sounds. Botox is made from botulinum toxin, which is also a deadly substance in other circumstances."

"Right," I said, my mind spinning. "So do they by any chance have to hurt the frogs to get the toxin from them?"

"The article doesn't say anything about how they get the toxin," Ned replied, sounding a little taken aback. "It's more about the possible uses of this stuff in makeup. But it does say that although the frog toxin acts similarly to Botox, there are some significant differences in the chemical structures of the two. Then there's a lot of technical stuff about what those differences are, which Vicente couldn't really explain."

BEEP! BEEP! My cell phone's battery alarm was going off. I winced as I realized I'd forgotten to charge it for the last two nights. "Sorry, I'm about to run out of juice," I told Ned.

"It's okay, I'm almost done. The gist of the article is that the author cautions that the frog toxin could be deadly over time, and that a ten-year study needs to be done to determine its long-term effects before it is put into use by the cosmetics industry."

A ten-year study. . . . I thought of what Piper had told me last night, about the e-mail her sister Robin had seen saying that more studies needed to be done on Perfect Face before it went on the market. The article I'd found in Anna's desk was from two years ago. So there was no way a ten-year study could have been completed by now.

Was that Kyle's secret? Was Perfect Face being made with an untested frog toxin?

BEEP! BEEP!

"Ned, I'd better go before we get cut off," I said. "Thanks, this is incredibly helpful. I'll explain it all to you when we have more time to talk."

"I'm looking forward to it," Ned said with a laugh. "But be careful, Nan, okay?"

"I always am. Bye, love you," I said, and hung up.

I sat there a moment longer, my mind racing. Things were starting to slot into place at last. I thought about the weird tingle I felt whenever I put the new Perfect Face on, and how I didn't feel it when I used the old version that Kelly used. In fact, Kyle had always made sure Kelly used the old version instead of the new.

I had that gut feeling that told me I was close to cracking this case. Yes, I was pretty sure now that I knew why Anna Chavez had had to disappear. . . .

But the most important question of all had yet to be answered:

Where was Anna Chavez now?

CLOSING IN ON THE TRUTH

I ran down to the business center and asked again if there were any faxes for me.

"No, Miss Drew," said the young woman behind the counter. "We have nothing for you."

"Could you do me a favor?" I asked. A scary thought had just occurred to me. "Could you check the log on that fax machine there?" I pointed to the one I had used last night. "It would have come through at about two a.m. and it would have been sent from a number with the River Heights area code." I handed her a scrap of paper on which I'd written down my area code at home.

"Of course." Giving me a puzzled look, the clerk went over and pressed some buttons on the fax machine. After a moment a list began printing out.

"Tell me," I said, struck by another thought, "are you the first person to come on duty at the business center this morning?"

"Yes, I am," she confirmed.

"Did this machine need to have paper loaded, or was it ready to go?"

The young woman wrinkled her brow as she thought. "It was full, I think. Yes, that's right, I didn't have to fill up any of the paper trays this morning. That's unusual—usually the last shift at night leaves everything all unprepared for the morning people." She put a hand over her mouth. "Oops. My boss's son works on the night shift. Can we just pretend I didn't say anything?"

"No problem," I assured her.

"Thanks." She scanned the log that had just printed out. "Oh, you're right, a fax did come in last night from that area code. Two pages came in at 2:13 a.m." She looked worried. "I can't understand what happened to it; it definitely wasn't here when I came on duty at six this morning."

"That's okay," I said. "I have a pretty good idea what happened to it." My stomach muscles had formed into a knot. I was thinking of Adam Bedrossian, standing in the lobby last night, watching me as I left the business center.

He must have loaded paper into the machine himself, waited around for my reply to come, and then intercepted it.

That meant two things to me: First, he was definitely in on whatever had happened to Anna. And, second, he knew exactly what I knew—so he'd be looking out for me.

That was a scary thought!

Thanking the woman behind the counter, I walked away and sank down on one of the lobby couches. What could I do next? I had a pretty good idea of why Anna had had to disappear, but no idea of how to find her.

Think, think. If I were Kyle McMahon, and I needed to get Anna out of the way in a hurry, what would I have done?

My guess was that Adam Bedrossian had actually done the dirty work, but even so, it seemed likely that Anna had to be somewhere in the city. Both Adam and Kyle had been around yesterday, so they really wouldn't have had time to take her anywhere far away.

That was, of course, assuming they didn't have other people working with them. On the whole, I thought that was unlikely. Kyle didn't strike me as the type to take unnecessary risks. And the more people there are involved in a criminal conspiracy, the riskier it is—the more chance it has of being exposed.

My hope was that Kyle believed that keeping Anna alive and unharmed was the least risky option for him. . . .

I shook my head. There was no point in thinking that way. I had to keep going on the assumption that Anna was still okay.

I cast my mind back over the last few days, trying to think of anything Kyle might have said that would give me a clue. . . .

And then I had it.

The new Pretty Face offices! They were housed in a brand-new building that wasn't yet occupied. It was also a place where no one would think twice about seeing Kyle McMahon or Adam Bedrossian. They could come and go without arousing any particular suspicion.

Could Anna be somewhere in that building?

Only one way to find out!

Jumping up, I ran outside and flagged down a yellow taxi. "I need to go to the Wall Street area," I told the driver. What street had Kyle said the new offices were on? "There's a new building being built somewhere on Albany—do you know where that is?"

The driver gave me a weary look. "I'll find it."

He turned south on a highway that ran down the west side of Manhattan and we were off.

Pulling out my phone, I began to compose a quick text to Bess and George. "Progress! Searching 4 Anna in new—"

That was as far as I got. My phone gave one final, outraged beep and the screen went dark. The battery was completely dead. Oh, no! I'd have to hope I could find a pay phone down at the building site.

The driver wove through a maze of small, hilly streets in far downtown Manhattan. Since it was a Saturday, the area was deserted—I guessed it wasn't very residential.

We passed an old-looking brown stone church and then the driver made a left. He pointed out his window. "This the place?"

I stared out at a brand-new, glass-and-steel office tower. There were big X-shapes taped on the plate-glass ground floor windows. Through them I could see a vast, empty lobby with a reception console below a mezzanine level filled with potted palms.

"I guess it is," I said. "Thanks."

I paid the driver and got out. I glanced around for a pay phone, but there were none in sight.

Well, I reasoned, even if Bess and George left Great-Aunt Estelle's and got here as fast as they could, it would still take them at least forty-five minutes—and those were minutes I didn't have to spare. I'd have to go in without backup.

Actually, I decided as I knocked on the glass, trying to attract the attention of the security guard who sat at the console inside, it was probably best that I was alone. It fit my cover story better.

After a moment or two he spotted me and ambled over to the door. Unlocking it, he drawled, "This building isn't open, Miss."

"I know," I said. I gave him my best smile. "I'm sorry to bother you. But I'm Kyle McMahon's assistant over at Pretty Face, and he sent me down here to pick up his cell phone. He thinks he left it up in the new offices yesterday."

The guard frowned. "Are you on my list?" he asked, holding up a clipboard.

"List?" I said, my heart sinking.

"I got a list of people who are authorized to come in here," the guard explained. "What's your name?" He began to turn pages, running a finger down the scrawled notes.

Uh-oh. "It's Nancy Drew, but I doubt I'm on there yet—I'm brand-new," I said. "I just started work this week." I tried the smile again. "I'd call

Mr. McMahon and have him vouch for me, but like I said, he lost his phone, so there's no way I can reach him."

"No, no Nancy Drew on here," the guard muttered, still scanning his list.

I glanced around the lobby, trying to see if there was any other way in. There had to be a fire exit, right? It looked like I was going to have to go to Plan B. Only I didn't exactly have a Plan B yet. . . .

The guard's finger suddenly stopped at an entry near the bottom of a page. "Wait a second. I got a note here that Mr. McMahon called. Says someone might be coming by to pick something up for him. That you?"

I almost laughed out loud. What a lucky coincidence! "Yes! That's me," I said.

"So he's got you working on a Saturday, huh? Man, that guy never stops. Okay. Come on in." The guard stepped back and let me past. At the security console, he handed me an electronic key card. "This'll get you through the internal doors. Go on up. Executive offices are on fifty. Take the west bank of elevators."

"Thank you." I took the card and headed around to the elevators, which were around the corner from the reception area.

The elevator came immediately and I stepped in. It went express to the thirtieth floor, then began to ping as it passed each story. I watched the red LED display. 32 . . . 33 . . . 34 . . . 35 . . .

That's about the first lucky break I've gotten on this case, I thought. I'd just have to be careful that I didn't run into whomever Kyle had actually sent down here. I wondered idly what he wanted picked up.

The doors slid open on the fiftieth floor. I stepped out, keyed myself into the foyer, and took a minute to admire the place.

The floors were covered with some sort of woven reed matting that was springy under my feet. Huge windows faced west, giving a spectacular view of the Hudson River, but I could tell from the smoky tint of the glass that they were coated with some kind of polarized covering so that the light could come in without the heat. I could see, too, that the building was cantilevered so that each floor stuck out a little bit beyond the one below it, creating a natural system of awnings.

There were lush plants everywhere, so that the place felt a bit like a tropical rain forest. They would take a lot of care, I guessed. But they would help keep the air inside fresh and cool. Kyle had been right. It really was a green building.

I shook my head. Pretty Face did seem like a great company in so many ways. It was a shame that its biggest success was founded on a lie. . . .

Now, to see if my hunch had been right.

I prowled down the halls of the fiftieth floor, peering into empty office after empty office. They were furnished already, with simple but elegant wooden desks and accessories. Everything was eerily silent.

I turned a corner. Now I was on the north side of the building. A corridor branched off from the center of that side, leading to a warren of internal offices. These didn't have windows, and even though the morning was sunny, they were extremely dark inside.

I opened a door and stuck my head into what seemed to be a small conference room. No Anna.

I walked on down the line. Office, office, office.

Then I opened the door to another conference room—and stopped short, my heart suddenly pounding. In the shadows I could just make out a figure slumped at the long conference table.

"Hello?" I called out.

The figure raised its head. *"Quién es?"* it murmured.

"Anna!" I cried. Throwing the door wide open, I ran forward. As my vision adjusted to the dimness, I could see that Anna appeared basically unhurt. But she was swaying in her seat and her eyes looked unfocused. Could she have been drugged?

She peered at me for a second, then frowned. "Nancy?" she slurred. "'Zat you?"

"Yes, it's me! I found you, Anna! I was so worried about you. Are you okay? What happened?" I blurted out.

Anna shook her head. "Satrap," she muttered.

"Huh?" Tucking my hand under her arm, I helped her to stand up. She sagged against me. "No, never mind, tell me later. For now, let's just get you out of here before the bad guys show up."

"Satrap," Anna said again. Raising her head with an effort, she said, "Too late." Her eyes went to a point over my shoulder. "It's . . . a . . . trap."

SATRAP!

Suddenly the light from the doorway was blocked out. I whirled around. Anna was right. It was a trap.

In the doorway stood Kyle McMahon. Behind him loomed the bulk of Adam Bedrossian. I couldn't see their faces until Kyle reached over and flicked the wall switch.

I stared at him and he stared at me. His face was white and strained.

"What are you doing here?" he demanded.

My pulse roared in my ears. Could I pull off a bluff? "I just wanted to see the offices," I tried. "I found Anna in here—I think she needs a doctor."

"Cut it out," Kyle snapped. "I know you lied your way in here looking for her. Adam said you would. He said you'd figured too much out."

I felt a jolt. So Adam and Kyle had set me up! "You called the guard and told him someone would be coming by and he should let them up," I said, realizing it hadn't been a coincidence after all.

"Adam did," Kyle said. "He figured if you'd made it this far, it would be easier to deal with you up here."

In a funny way, the knowledge that I couldn't bluff them made me feel calmer. I had nothing more to lose. Beside me, Anna sat down with a soft groan.

"Oh, this is no good," Kyle moaned. He began to pace up and down. "This is bad, bad. For goodness' sake, Nancy, why couldn't you leave well enough alone?"

"I'm sorry," I retorted, "but the fact that Anna disappeared suddenly, without a trace, wasn't something I could just 'leave alone.'"

"Yes, yes, very heroic," he snapped, waving a hand at me as he continued to pace. "Everyone else accepted the cover story, why couldn't you?"

"I guess I just have a suspicious nature," I said. "And there were all the little things that didn't add up.

"So tell me if I missed anything," I went on. I gestured at Adam. "I know you intercepted the fax that was supposed to come to me this morning."

Adam nodded. His deadpan manner seriously creeped me out.

"I know about the Venezuelan frog toxin. Anna did some research on the frog and became concerned that the company hadn't run tests on the long-term effects of the toxin on people's nervous systems. That's what she wanted to talk to me about, isn't it?"

"That's right," Kyle acknowledged. "She'd been badgering me about it for months, ever since she happened across some article in an old scientific journal. I thought I'd finally gotten her to drop it. But then when those crazy protesters showed up, Anna started up again. She said that what we were doing was the same thing, morally speaking, as testing our products on animals. I ask you! I mean, this stuff is perfect—it's a true miracle substance. And it's one hundred percent natural. We are doing women of the world a huge favor by giving them Perfect Face!"

"You mean you're doing your company a huge favor," I pointed out. "Perfect Face makes millions of dollars a year for you. If you had to pull it off the market for testing, Pretty Face cosmetics would probably go under."

"It's possible to make products that are good for business *and* good for the consumer. And the environment as well," Kyle insisted. "That's Pretty Face's core philosophy. And Perfect Face is good for the consumer and the environment. We don't even harm the frogs to get the toxin. All we do is harvest their shed skins." He turned to Anna. "How could you think I was trying to hurt anyone?" he asked her. "That hurts me!"

He sounded genuinely upset.

Anna peered up at him, her eyelids heavy. "Need . . . to test it," she said stubbornly. "You don't know...what could happen over time."

"But the native tribes in that part of Venezuela have been using it medicinally for centuries!"

"Not the same," Anna replied. Her voice sounded stronger, to my relief. Whatever she was doped up with, maybe it was starting to wear off. "There are many differences, the main one being they don't use it every single day. They use it as a painkiller or an anesthetic when they need it. Anyway, who knows what the long-term effects on the natives are? No one has ever studied it."

Kyle scowled. "You're being needlessly academic. We have enough evidence without doing a formal ten-year study. It's just not necessary—common sense will tell you that!"

"If you're so convinced your product is safe," I spoke up, "then why don't you let your own daughter use it? Why do you keep giving Kelly the old formulation of Perfect Face?"

Kyle winced and was silent.

"I thought so," I said, folding my arms.

All this time Adam Bedrossian had been standing impassively by the doorway. Now he spoke for the first time.

"Kyle," he rumbled, "we're wasting time with all this chitchat. Let's get on with what we have to do."

Kyle's face looked haggard. "We can't," he said with a touch of desperation. "For heaven's sake, Adam, we can't go that far—we're businessmen!"

My lungs suddenly felt as if all the air had been pressed out of them. Was Adam planning to get rid of me and Anna?

"We don't have a choice," Adam said. For the first time since I'd met him, I heard a hint of emotion in his voice—impatience. "Think about it. We crossed the line when we first brought Anna here against her will. Once we'd done that, surely you could see that there was only one way it could end. We couldn't let her go after that."

"That isn't true!" I said quickly. Maybe I could appeal to Kyle's better nature. "Kyle, if you harm us, you will get caught. It's just a matter of time. My friends know everything that I know"— mentally I crossed my fingers—"and if I disappear, they'll know who to blame. But this can still have a happy ending. All you have to do is announce a voluntary recall of Perfect Face. If you do that, you'll look like heroes for pulling the product off the shelves before there are any complaints about it. And Anna and I will promise to keep quiet."

Adam chuckled. "Nice try, Miss Drew."

I ignored him and stared at Kyle, willing him to agree. But to my dismay, his expression hardened and he shook his head.

"We can't pull Perfect Face off the market," he insisted. "It's out of the question."

"Like I said, there's only one way this can end," Adam drawled. Stepping toward me, his hand suddenly shot out with startling speed and grabbed my arm. I tried my best to pull free, but his grip was like iron—there was no way I could break it. He hauled me out of the conference room and toward a fire exit.

"Come on, Kyle," he called over his shoulder.

"You should be able to handle Anna on your own. The chopper's waiting on the roof."

Chopper! Where were they taking us?

As Adam pulled me up the stairs to the roof, I struggled as hard as I could. But it was like trying to fight with an iron statue. He didn't even break his stride.

Throwing open the door to the roof, he stepped out, pulling me behind him. Wind whipped my hair into my eyes and the sudden sunlight dazzled me.

A small helicopter sat on a landing pad at the far end of the roof, its rotors turning slowly. Adam lifted me bodily into the cabin, strapped me into a seat, then calmly pulled out a pair of handcuffs and cuffed my hands in front of me. He reached under the seat and pulled out a coil of rope, which he used to tie my legs to the seat supports.

I sat there, helpless, shards of icy fear stabbing at my heart.

Anna was bundled into a seat beside me and tied up the same way I was. Then Kyle climbed into the copilot seat and Adam took the controls. "Keep an eye on them," he shouted to Kyle over the roar of the rotors. "*Especially* Miss Drew."

A moment later the chopper rose into the air.

It banked and began to fly north, up the Hudson River. I sat there, staring down blankly at the silvery ribbon of water. No one had any idea where I had gone. My cell phone was dead, so even if I had been able to reach it, there was no possibility of using it to call for help. I had no idea where we were going.

For some reason, at that moment, the Miss Pretty Face pageant popped into my mind. It was tonight—only about eight hours from now.

Looks like I'm going to miss it, I reflected bleakly. I guess Piper was going to get her shot at the crown after all.

I'd been in tight spots plenty of times before, but this was the worst yet. And, unfortunately for Anna and me, I was fresh out of tricks.

How, how, *how* was I going to get us out of this one?

THE HARDY BOYS

BOYS

They've got motorcycles,
their cases are ripped from the headlines,
and they work for ATAC:
American Teens Against Crime.

CRIMINALS, BEWARE:

THE HARDY BOYS ARE ON YOUR TRAIL!

Frank and Joe tell all-new stories of crime,

danger, death-defying stunts, mystery, and teamwork.

Ready? Set? Fire it up!

She's sharp.

She's smart.

She's confident.

She's unstoppable.

And she's on your trail.

Still sleuthing,

still solving crimes,

but she's got some new tricks up her sleeve!

NANCY DREW

girl detective

 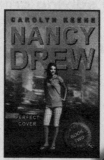